The Goat, the Sofa
and
Mr Swami

R Chandrasekar was born in Madras and
studied at Mayo College, Vivekananda College
Madras, the Delhi School of Economics and the
University of Chicago. He has researched and
priced commodities and derivatives, traded bonds,
managed portfolios, taught, and run a financial
research centre. Chandrasekar lives with his family
in the city formerly known as Madras. This is his
first novel.

The Goat, the Sofa
and
Mr Swami

R. Chandrasekar

First published in book form in 2010 by Hachette India
An Hachette UK company

SRD

**This is a work of fiction. Any resemblance to real
persons, living or dead, is purely coincidental.**

Hachette India
612/614 (6th Floor), Time Tower,
MG Road, Sector 28, Gurgaon-122001, India

Typeset in Cochin 11/13.5
Mindways Design, New Delhi

Printed and bound in India by
Manipal Technologies Limited, Manipal

MIX
Paper from
responsible sources

FSC
www.fsc.org   FSC™ C104740

For Ambika
without whose insistence
this would never have been completed
and for Vishwanath
who insists that he could have come up
with a better title for it

1

An Invitation

1

'Sir?'

There was no movement.

I could just about see his head as he sat slouched down in front of the television.

It has always been thus.

He waddles back from the cabinet meeting muttering profanities, waddles over to the liquor cabinet, unlocks it (he is notably distrustful, you see), and carries the large two-litre bottle of Red Label to the sofa. It's up to me to provide the rest – ice, soda, glass, glasses.

He never wears his glasses in public, not even at cabinet meetings, but the fact is that he can barely see without them. There was this embarrassing incident the previous week when he pinched the bottom of the agriculture minister. Nothing terribly wrong there in principle, I admit. The old fart deserved to get his arse pinched – and also have his balls squeezed while the prime-ministerial fingers were doing their bit – being a lecher and a paedophile when not tending to Indian agriculture. However, the intended target of the Old Man's attentions was not the seventy-three-year-old, fat and balding krishi mantri, but the minister of state – independent charge – of tourism: forty-four, slim, lustrous-locked and female.

I'm also expected to provide a cushion for those wobbly legs to rest on, to turn on the television and DVD player and put on the DVD of a popular film starring the Choli Girl, and which has her dancing nude. (She didn't actually dance nude, but the head of a software company that needed a few strings pulled by the PMO had his people undress her digitally, allowing the Old Man to watch the film unencumbered by the heroine's clothes.)

In case you were wondering, I am Swamy, IAS, joint secretary in the PMO. The Old Man is the Prime Minister and he was watching the scene where the Choli Girl wiggles her hips – you know, the bit that got M.F. Husain all excited. If you've seen the scene and tried to imagine it with a bare derriere, you will understand my reluctance to interrupt as well as the lack of response from the Old Man. But I had little choice.

'Sir,' I said a little more loudly, edging closer.

No response. The music blared on. One of the sexiest heroines of Hindi cinema danced and sang with no clothes on. It was highly erotic. The Old Man thought so as well. His pyjama was open and his fingers were attempting to coax life into his eighty-two-year-old penis. I looked away, looked at the TV screen and cleared my throat.

His instructions to me were very clear: pour me my drink, put on the movie and clear out. He had an electric bell handy to summon me, which he invariably used only as the movie drew to a close, with the demurely clad heroine bound in matrimony. The digital artists had allowed her this final shred of dignity. Invariable, too, was the dazed, somewhat dishevelled look, the hastily tied pyjama, the added wobble to his waddle, as he made his way to his bedroom in a trance. There was a framed picture there of his late wife at which he never looked. Perhaps he wished to carry with him the image of the Choli Girl unsullied by more earthbound memories.

Perhaps, too, he was too preoccupied by affairs of state to notice.

Affairs of state were far from his mind now. I had edged around to try and catch his eye. There was a manic look there as he took in the show.

'Sir!' I almost shouted. What I wanted most of all then was a quick trip to the loo. The PM was a most un-grandfatherly eighty-two year old, at least to the minions who had to tend to him, quite in contrast to the avuncular attitude he affected in public.

He glared at me.

I quailed.

'What is this? What is this?' His penis rapidly retreated to a quiescent state.

'Sorry, sir. Telephone call.'

'Telephone call? Telephone call?' He was prone in his dotage to repeat himself.

I nodded.

'Telephone call?' The Choli Girl danced on, unknowing and uncaring. 'Who do you think I am, Swamy? A chaprasi?'

'No, sir, you are the Prime Minister of India.'

'And you want me to answer a telephone call?'

'I'm sorry, sir, but it is the Prime Minister of Pakistan on the line.'

'Hain? Why does that son of a swine have to call at this time? Doesn't he know that... that... that I'm busy at this time? Who is our ambassador there?'

'Vikram Kapoor, sir.'

'Sack him. Can't he tell that bloody idiot that I'm always busy at this time?'

'Perhaps he didn't know, sir.'

'Perhaps? *Perhaps?* What is this perhaps? You mean you didn't *tell* him?'

'Sir,' I glanced at the screen. 'How could I tell him?'

'Ullu ke patthe! Gadhe! You should have sent a memo to all concerned, stating that the PM is busy and not to be disturbed at this hour. Not to be disturbed at this hour, samjhe?'

'Sir, the Pakistani PM is still waiting.'

'Bewaqoof! I will sack you.'

I finally found my tongue. 'Sorry, sir, but you cannot.'

'Hain? Hain?'

'My appointment falls under the IAS appointment rules. I can be transferred – not sacked.'

'Then I will transfer you to Jhumritalayya.'

'Sorry, sir, but I can revert only to my home state.'

'Home state? Home state?'

'The Pakistani PM is still waiting, sir.'

'Bloody fool!' He glared at me, stole a longing look at the TV screen. 'Get me the bloody phone then.'

2

'Prime Minister of India speaking.'

The Old Man had a voice, not always evident when the Choli Girl occupied his thoughts and loins, but there as part of his armoury nonetheless, which carried a certain weight, a gravitas that was most apposite to the events of state he was expected to grace. Amitabh Bachchan with added dignity and wisdom. Sivaji Ganesan in his mythological avatar, but sans the cheap alliterations. A voice befitting a statesman. A voice that had brought him to the pinnacle of Indian politics.

A voice, I have to admit, that reminded me that I was a fringe participant in the making of history.

On the fringes, I listened in on an extension line.

'Keshavji, salaam aleikum.'

'Namaste.' The voice was frigid in its gravity, the interruption not forgotten.

'Bhaisahib, gal sunao. Kudi-vudi hai aapke saath?'

'Hain, hain? I am eighty-two years old.' I sensed a tremor of uncertainty in the Voice.

'Arre, so what? Age is no barrier.'

'How do *you* know?'

A chuckle came over the line. 'My father is eighty years old. No good Pakistani nurse will stay more than two days with him. Very naughty man. So, we have to get nurses from Bangladesh.'

'But why Bangladesh? I hear there are very nice nurses to be had in Thailand and Laos.'

'True, very true. I investigated myself on my last visit there...'

'But my intelligence fellows told me you were meeting with the Bodo people.'

'You really believe everything your intelligence fellows tell you? Bhaisahib, I shall tell you something. I gave your intelligence fellows the slip. Needed some privacy to check out the nurses there, heh, heh, heh. But bhaisahib, a fully wasted trip.'

'Fully wasted? A young man like you? A good Punjab da puttar? What is this you are saying?'

'No, no, you are misunderstanding fully. Equipment check all okay – first class even. But my father wants only Muslim nurses. It makes it very difficult. Have to dress them up as camel jockeys and send them through Dubai. Complicated business.'

'Why not Indonesian nurses?'

'Keshavji, you are a genius! An absolute genius!'

'Eighty-two years old, PM of a hundred crore people – it keeps me on my toes.'

'And Amitabh Bachchan movies, no doubt.'

'Amitabh Bachchan?'

'Heh, heh heh. My little secret. You see, my intelligence fellows tell me you watch Amitabh Bachchan movies each night.'

Much coughing from the PM – our PM, that is. 'You really believe everything your intelligence fellows tell you? I too can give them the slip. Actually, I watch Kurosawa movies, but only once or twice a week.'

'Kurosawa? That *Last Tango* fellow? You have that movie?'

'Not *that* Kurosawa. You tell your intelligence fellows to do their job properly. All this dancing stuff is not for me. Anyway, this is a most enjoyable conversation, but surely you were not calling just to say hello?'

'But why not? We must chat from time to time. One thing, though. There is a cricket test match in Delhi next month. Wonder if you can invite me?'

'Invite? Of course, why not? But you will need hotel reservations and all, na? Let me see. No paper-pencil here. Wait. I need to write down how many in your party. My memory is not so good these days, you see. Eighty-two years and all that and every night, my late wife insists on interrupting my dreams. Bloody headache, if you ask me...'

'Keshavji, you have your Vikram Kapoor. I have my Fazlur Rehman. Let the bloody diplomats do some bloody work for a change.'

'Good idea, yes. That nincompoop Kapoor never does any work. Always unprepared. Very difficult for me.'

'One more thing, Keshavji. This has been a private conversation, na?'

'Of course, of course.'

'So I will be seeing you in Delhi in due course?'

'Of course, of course.'

'And you can show me some of that Kurosawa fellow's movies?'

'Kurosawa? Oh yes. Oh yes. Of course, of course. Khuda hafiz. Namaste. Good night.'

I heard the sound of the leaders hanging up and was doing so most carefully myself when I heard the PM hollering from the next room:

'Swamy, you too can hang up now. Go find out where I can get Kurosawa movies.'

3

A simple matter, as I've already told you, and the IFS bastards still go and bugger things up. Well, not entirely their fault, but Vikram Kapoor certainly deserves to carry the can on this one.

Here's what happened.

Our PM, well fuelled by Red Label and thoughts of the Choli Girl, dropped off into deep slumber without mentioning the phone call to anyone. I knew about it, yes, but since I was not supposed to be eavesdropping, I did not know about it officially (even if the PM knew, unofficially, that I had been eavesdropping). And if I didn't know about it officially, I could hardly be expected to do anything about it. In any event, it was late in the evening, the test match more than a month away, a sense of urgency entirely absent.

The Pakistani PM being so much younger (remember his randy father?) evidently felt he needed to get a move on. He called a press conference (try that late in the evening with our press!) and announced that he had accepted the Indian PM's invitation to the test match. Responding to a question, he expressed a desire to see all the test matches – the one in Delhi *and* the ones in Itanagar and Tirunelveli. Provided, of course, that there was no objection from the Indian side. All very correct and unexceptional – nothing that I could find fault with, at any rate.

Unaware of all this, the Indian side snored on.

The Pakistani press made a beeline for Vikram Kapoor's house. Roused from a moment of intimacy with his bibi, clad in banian and striped knickers, he opened the door to be greeted by flashbulbs and TV cameras. Asked about the invitation, he responded like a true lathi-up-his-arse IFS type: 'There has been no invitation to the Prime Minister of Pakistan to visit India nor is there any invitation planned.' He went on to add some twaddle about the Shimla Declaration, but this was lost in the loud hubbub that followed his statement.

The Pakistani press went to town with this sensational development. So did BBC, CNN, CNBC and NDTV. The shit had well and truly hit the fan.

What made things worse was that there was no one to respond from our side. Our foreign minister was spending the night in a ger somewhere in Mongolia, the minister of state was holidaying in Amsterdam and had switched off his mobile, the deputy minister had been ordered to stay away from the ministry and not speak a word out of turn, the bureaucrats would say nothing of substance. There was plenty on the Shimla Declaration, nothing on the cricket match.

The Pakistanis had won the media war by a knockout.

4

The PM had made it clear that he was to be woken up only in the event of war.

There was no war, so I did not wake him up when the Pakistani PM called. There was no war, so he woke up at his usual time of nine or so. There was no war, so he had his bath, his morning prayers and his breakfast (aloo parathas with ghee, hot jalebis and a glass of sweet lassi) undisturbed. He then settled down to watch the Tom and Jerry show, something he enjoyed and appreciated immensely. Half an hour of this and I felt that he was ready to face the newspapers. It was past eleven in the morning.

He disliked reading and it was my job to read him the news I considered important. I must admit that I did not look forward to this on that particular morning. I suppose I could have skipped the bit about the cricket match, but he would have learned about it at some point and then it would have been up shit creek for me. He can be a formidable old SOB when he chooses and I've yet to figure out how best to handle him. I took a deep breath and plunged into the news.

Indo-Pak Relations Hit a New Low
By Our Correspondent

Relations between India and Pakistan, touchy in the best of times, spiralled to a new low over something as mundane as a cricket match. It will be recalled that the Pakistan team is due to play three tests in India in a month's time. At a hastily called press conference last night, the Prime

Minister of Pakistan, Mr Hafez Ali Shah, announced that he had accepted an invitation from the Prime Minister of India, Mr Keshavchand Motwani, to witness the test match in Delhi.

Mr Shah went on to express his desire to watch the other two tests as well, to be held in Itanagar, Arunachal Pradesh, and Tirunelveli in Tamil Nadu.

Contacted by the press, the Indian ambassador here, Mr Vikram Kapoor, denied that any invitation had been extended by the Indians. 'There has been no invitation to the Prime Minister of Pakistan to visit India nor is there any invitation planned,' he said.

He went on to accuse the Pakistan government of violating the spirit of the Shimla Agreement of 1972. Asked to elaborate, he stated that Mr Shah's statement was 'a cheap stunt aimed at embarrassing the Indian government'. He added that a visit 'could only come about after elaborate consultations on both sides' and that 'there were no plans to hold such consultations now or in the future'.

A spokesman for the foreign ministry in New Delhi elaborated on the consultative mechanism set up as part of the Shimla Agreement and stated that Pakistan had violated it.

Mr Shah expressed dismay when told of the Indian reaction:

'All I want to do is watch the cricket match. Sports can help ease the tensions between our countries and I was hoping to cheer both sides on the field. The Prime Minister of India was very positive in welcoming me. It appears that he has changed his mind. Doubtless there are hardliners in the Indian government who want to discourage any move towards peace. I am sorry that Mr Motwani has given in to them. This will not help the cause of peace. I have no intention of going to India under the current circumstances.'

While the sequence of events remains unclear, with each side accusing the other of falsehoods and duplicity, what is clear is that relations between the traditional enemies have touched a new low.

I cleared my throat and waited for the explosion. It came.

'What is this nonsense? What is this rubbish? What is that idiot Kapoor talking about? I have invited Shah. I am the Prime Minister of India. I will transfer him to Jhumritalayya.'

It was not the moment to remind him that IFS officers cannot be transferred to Jhumritalayya. It was not the moment to speak or comment. It was a moment to stand silently.

I stood silently.

'Well, what are you waiting for? Call up Kapoor and tell him to pack up his bags.'

I couldn't very well do that. These IFS chaps can be oversensitive; their dealings with us are prickly even at the best of times.

'Sir, the service rules of the Government of India...'

'You think I am a fool? Mujhe ulloo samajhte ho?'

'Certainly not, sir. You are like a respected grandfather to me.'

'I am like your grandfather? What was your grandfather?'

'Which one, sir?'

'You idiot! Talking back to me like this? Any grandfather. All grandfathers.'

'Sir, one was an assistant station-master and the other worked in a mental asylum.'

'You are calling me a mad station-master? I am a freedom fighter, you understand, a freedom fighter. I get a freedom fighter's pension from the government. While your bloody grandfather was working for the British, I was fighting for India's independence.'

Taking abuse from politicians is part of the job, but having one's ancestors insulted is not. It was a difficult moment for me, but I knew deep within that I had to do what I had to do.

'My grandfathers were honourable gentlemen, sir, unlike some assistant village munsifs serving under the British that I know of who were caught stealing dhotis and put into prison. I shall be resigning from the IAS, sir, in view of the gratuitous insults I have had to put up with, and once relieved from service, shall hold a press conference explaining in detail the reasons for the extreme step I have been forced to take.'

'How do you know about all that?' His face was suddenly ashen.

'All what, sir?' Time to string the bastard along.

'What you were just saying. Just saying, you know what.'

'You know what what, sir?'

'Arre, surely you are understanding, that what, you know what?'

'What what, sir?'

He wrung his hands. 'The assistant munsif bit, that's what.'

'My grandfathers were honest gentlemen, sir.'

'Just a joke, you are understanding, just a joke.'

'A very poor joke, sir.'

'Yes, yes, a very poor joke indeed. But how come we are talking about these very honourable gentlemen, your grandfathers?'

'Conversations sometimes meander, sir, like the river Ganga.'

'Yamuna as well. As also the Narmada, Godavari, et cetera, et cetera. All meandering.'

'Yes, sir.'

'Tell me, is this Leander also meandering?'

'I don't understand, sir.'

'This tennis player, Leander. Why is he called Leander?'

'I have an idea sir.'

'You know why Leander is called Leander?'

'I have no idea, sir.'

'But you just said that you have an idea. You are confusing me now.'

'An idea, sir, but not about Leander. You see, the Pakistanis might beat us in cricket. Not good if Mr Shah is watching. So why don't we challenge them to a tennis match? That way, if Leander is playing, we will beat them.'

'A tennis match, eh? What a good idea! I will invite Shah myself.'

'Sir...'

'What is it now?'

'About that cricket match...'

'Oh yes. The cricket match. What will that Shah think?'

'He called last night, sir. Perhaps you should return the call.'

'I know he called last night. I spoke to him.'

'Sir, he called once again. After Kapoor spoke to the press.'

'Why wasn't I told?'

'You had given instructions not to be disturbed unless there was a war. There was no war. However, if you feel that I erred, I will not hesitate to resign, sir.'

'No, no, no. Don't resign. I've already told you, your grandfathers were very honourable. Good patriots. No need to resign. No. Now get me Shah on the phone.'

5

'Arre, Shah sahib, salaam aleikum. I was told that you called last night. But I was fast asleep. Not to be disturbed, the doctors said. I am now eighty-two years old, you see.'

The Pakistani PM's voice was utterly lacking in bonhomie and good cheer.

Cold, in a word.

'Mr Prime Minister, I have been embarrassed and humiliated. I have had to face my citizens and explain myself. I am upset, my country has been insulted. There is nothing more to talk about.'

'Arre, don't be upset. You will be my guest here. I will chastize that Kapoor. Ulloo ka pattha! I am transferring him to Jhumritalayya.'

'You cannot transfer him to Jhumritalayya. He is IFS.'

'How do you know all this?'

'I have my sources. Anyway, you can transfer him to Mogadishu.'

'What is that?'

'A country in Africa – people shooting each other all the time.'

'Good suggestion. How do you spell it? Wait, wait, let me find a pen. Always when you are looking for a pen, you never find it. Arre Swami! One minute, Mr Shah. Swami, get me a pen. Good, now tell me.'

'M-O- G- A- D –I- S- H- U.'

'In Africa, you say?'

'Yes. And Keshavji, this Kapoor is always going on about Shimla.'

'I know. These IFS fellows are always going on about Shimla.'

'You agree that this is all rubbish?'

'Of course, of course.'

'Keshavji, you are a gentleman.'

'Thank you, thank you.'

The Old Man was obviously exceeding his brief. I waved my hands frantically to get his attention.

'One minute, this Swami is waving. Oh yes, the tennis match. Shah sahib, I invite you – Pakistan, that is – for a tennis match here. Leander and all will play. We can both watch.'

'Tennis match? Good idea. I will consult with the generals and get back to you.'

I continued to try to catch the Old Man's eye. 'This Swami is still waving. Another phone call, I think.'

'So, Keshavji, you will call a press conference and clarify things?'

'Of course, of course. Khuda hafiz.'

'Sir, you should never have said that!' I said as he hung up.

The Old Man looked at me quizzically. 'It was your idea about the tennis match. Now you are telling me that I should never have said that?'

'Not that, sir. Shimla.'

'Now IAS also. Always the IFS fellows are talking about Shimla. Shimla is a rubbish place. Not like the old days. Have you been there recently?'

2

The Press Conference

1

People often talk of the good old days when Nehru held impromptu press conferences. These people forget that Nehru was an old Harrovian and a Cambridge man to boot. His life contained its share of surprising turns, but a wayside halt as assistant village munsif was not one of them. Neither was a stint in the can for stealing the munsif's dhotis.

The Old Man was apt to go shooting off his mouth – witness his exchange with that crafty old so-and-so, Shah. His press conferences had to be meticulously organized: the press briefed, experts lined up to help him avoid minefields, experts lined up to help him *recognize* the minefields, makeup artists to help hide his age – in other words, the works. Spontaneity is all very fine in theory, but has no place in practical politics. Getting the machinery up and running was like getting a DTC bus to move.

There was also this business of Shah to consider.

On past form, his press conference was likely already under way. I've always envied our Pakistani counterparts. A pliant press, a pliant legislature, a PM not in his dotage, a single point agenda (the K word, in case you were wondering), the bastards could – and did – hold press conferences with Nehruvian frequency. The press has really no business criticizing the IAS for being slow to react. After all, we didn't vote for the Old Man. At least, I didn't and you can't blame me for having to waste time cleaning up after him.

I did the best I could under the circumstances – announce that a press conference would be held shortly and that the subject was the Pakistani PM's upcoming visit to watch the Delhi test match.

Just as well.

As I anticipated, Shah held his press conference, announcing with glee that the Indians were no longer holding Pakistan to the Shimla Agreement and that the Indian high commissioner was being recalled in deference to Pakistan's wishes.

Cheeky bastards.

2

I have to hand it to the Old Man, though. Once briefed, and having had the consequences of certain loose utterances pointed out to him, he held forth with panache and a certain je ne sais quoi. There were times when I could see why the good folk of Jhumritalayya voted for him and his ilk in large numbers.

He spoke in Hindi of course and this is a translation: 'Ladies and gentlemen, a very good evening to you. I am happy to inform you that the Prime Minister of Pakistan, Mr Hafez Ali Shah, has accepted my invitation to attend the test match between India and Pakistan to be held in New Delhi shortly. Mr Shah, as you know, is a keen follower of cricket and it is my privilege and pleasure to have him here to enjoy the game. I hope that his family will accompany him and avail of our hospitality. The details of his visit will be announced after consultations between the two governments. Thank you for your time.'

As anticipated, the press wasn't going to let him get away with a bland statement like that. There was a chorus of shouts and much waving of hands. We had arranged for a few questions from some friendly journalists and the PM duly singled out one of them.

'Sir, were there any other matters discussed with Mr Shah?'

'Yes, yes. Mr Shah wanted to see a few movies when he visits.'

'Any movies in particular, sir?'

'Arre, that very famous one. *Last Tango in Paris*. That one.'

An explosion of feeling and thoughts. An excited buzz. Take that, Shah.

'A clarification, sir. You said *Last Tango in Paris*? With Marlon Brando and Maria Schneider?'

'Yes, indeed.'

'Is this going to be a special screening, sir?'

'We in India have an ancient tradition of hospitality. Our guests' slightest whim is our command. We will bow to Shah sahib's wishes.'

'Any other matters, sir?'

'Yes. I invited the Prime Minister to bring a tennis team over as well. We wish to broaden the contacts between our people.'

'Has an agreement been reached on this as well?'

'Not yet. Mr Shah informed me that he needs the concurrence of the Pakistani army before accepting my invitation.'

Another loud buzz of excitement. Shah was going to rue the day he tried to pull a fast one on us. This was going well.

Time now for a few hostile questions.

The lady from the BBC was almost falling over in her attempt to catch the Old Man's eye. He gestured in her direction.

'Sir, in his press conference earlier today, Mr Shah said – quote – the Indian Prime Minister and I have agreed that the Shimla Declaration of 1972 should no longer govern negotiations between our countries – unquote. Yet just yesterday, the spokesman from your foreign ministry as well as your high commissioner in Pakistan referred to the consultative mechanism laid out in the Shimla Declaration. What, sir, is the position of the Indian government?'

'Where did you study?'

'I beg your pardon, sir?'

'Arre, simple question only. Where did you study?'

The poor thing looked thoroughly confused. Everyone was staring at her. She went pale, then pink. 'Leeds University, sir. But I fail to understand...'

'Not Oxford? Not Cambridge? Never mind. You still speak English very beautifully. And you are very beautiful as well.'

Not quite. She looked more like a horse, if you ask me. A very flustered horse. 'Well, thank you very much for your compliment, sir.'

Titters all around.

She glared at the titterers.

They felt silent.

'Any more questions?' asked the Old Man.

Ms Beeb remembered once more who she was, where she was. Poor thing – it must have been the first time she had been called beautiful. That sort of thing can reduce the sharpest of minds to jelly.

'You haven't answered my question, sir.'

'Oh yes, your question. You see, Mr Shah seems to have misunderstood part of our conversation.

We merely agreed that these days there is a lot of rubbish in Shimla – a real problem. But the Congress government in Himachal is refusing to do anything about it. A real scandal, if you ask me. We must do more for the environment.'

One could sense the confusion among the scribes. The Old Man had successfully muddied the waters.

'A follow-up question, sir.' This was the CNN man.

'Yes?'

'Mr Shah also mentioned that you had agreed to transfer your high commissioner in Pakistan.'

'Mr Shah seems to have mentioned a lot of things.'

'Is his statement correct, sir?'

The Old Man gave a theatrical sigh. 'I am the Prime Minister of India. I am responsible for the welfare of a hundred crore people. Do you really think that I spend my time discussing the transfer of individual officers? And with the Pakistani Prime Minister at that? Surely Mr Shah has misunderstood our conversation. Perhaps when he comes here on his visit, I will advise him to privatize his telephone company. It improves sound quality in my opinion.'

'But, sir, he stated very clearly that Mr Kapoor was to be transferred to Mogadishu.'

'You are misunderstanding things. You see, Mr Shah wanted to know where Mogadishu was.

I informed him that it was in Africa. Then I wanted to know why he needed this information. He said that his high commissioner here wanted a transfer to Mogadishu. As a joke, I told him that, perhaps, Kapoor can go there too. It seems there are lots of gangsters there. Perhaps he misunderstood the joke. No more questions, I hope.'

'Sir, one last question. Last night, Mr Shah expressed a desire to see the other test matches, too. Will he be attending the matches in Itanagar and Tirunelveli as well?'

'I must say that this desire was not conveyed to me personally. In the event that a formal request is conveyed, either to me personally or through official channels, we shall have to consider security and other aspects. We shall make known our response after due consideration of these matters. Now, thank you and good night.'

3

Other aspects. Now why did those damn fools in the BCCI decide to hold test matches in Itanagar and Tirunelveli of all places? We all know the official excuses – the need to popularize the sport, the need to keep spectators around the country involved, the need to tire out visiting teams by having them gallivant all around the country. All old chestnuts thrown at us year after year. We also know the real reason – keeping the regional satraps in good humour. We've had matches in Cuttack, Guwahati, Indore and various other garden spots. But Itanagar? Give us all a break.

And now that Shah had expressed a desire to be at these places, the Intelligence Bureau, a paranoid lot at the best of times, had gone completely ballistic.

A short primer in geopolitics is in order here. Itanagar is in Arunachal Pradesh, bordering China (okay, Tibet). For reasons known only to them (rooted in dialectics and Mao Zedong thought, no doubt) the Chinese have decided that it belongs to them. The Chinese are apt to do this sort of thing. They claim that Tibet and all of the South China Sea belong to them. What all of this means is that Arunachal Pradesh is a Sensitive Area, capitals intended. So, we can't have all and sundry traipsing around there as if in their backyard. And certainly not someone like Shah, who can't keep his trap shut and buys missiles from the Chinese in his spare time.

The fact is that the IB officials know they have numerous chinks in their armour and have good reason to be paranoid about the proposed visit.

There was something else as well.

Tirunelveli, the site of the third test match, was too close to LTTE territory for comfort. It was also too close to a big nuclear power plant we were building with Russian help. Not the sort of place to have running around the ISI types that would naturally accompany Shah.

As cock-ups go, this one was in the major league.

4

Being the PM's private secretary has its attractions. People assume that you are privy to all the intrigue and politics swirling around 7 Race Course Road.

I do nothing to disabuse them of the notion.

Fazlur Rehman had called thrice by the time I returned from the press conference. He was in a state, to put it mildly.

'Swami!' The agitation in his voice came through loud and clear: 'What is this your PM is talking about?'

I feigned ignorance. 'He is a loquacious sort, isn't he? To which utterance might you be alluding, my dear Fazlur?'

Fazlur was a good decade or so older than me, an Oxford man and my senior in rank. Another day, another time, and I might well have been kissing his arse, but not now. As I said, being the PM's private secretary has its attractions and I could afford the easy familiarity, the turns of phrase one gentleman adopts with another.

'You were at the press conference, weren't you? The bit about my wanting to go to Mogadishu.'

'Yes?'

'I mean, I don't want to go to Mogadishu. Who the hell *wants* to go to Mogadishu?'

'I'm told that the Indian Ocean is quite balmy at times.'

'Come off it, will you? Did Shah tell Motwani that he wanted me transferred to Mogadishu?'

'How would I know, Fazlur?'

'We all know that you listen in on the PM's calls.'

'I'm afraid that you are suffering from some delusion.'

'The ISI is never wrong.'

'Then why don't you ask your bloody ISI what Shah told Motwani? And while you are at it, ask them where they got the idea that Motwani watches Amitabh Bachchan movies.'

'Listen, Swami. Damn it. You know the fix I am in.'

'I suppose you could ask your ISI to unfix it.'

'Okay, okay, my apologies. I should never have brought the ISI into it.'

'Well then, is there anything else?'

'Have a word with Motwani, Swami. Have him put in a good word for me. Mogadishu? Hell.'

He was probably right, but that did not prevent a little diplomatic contretemps.

5

'Swami, this is Neeta Kochar.'

Neeta minds the store over at External Affairs and is their liaison officer with the PMO.

'Yes, Neeta?'

'We have a little problem here.'

'So what's new? Did you watch the press conference? Wasn't the Old Man great?'

'Shah and his buddies don't like shit being flung in their faces like this.'

'Serve him right after what he did to us.'

'We must be careful. There could be another coup there.'

'Big deal! Doesn't seem to make a whole lot of difference in the way they behave.'

'Oh no, there are any number of nuances that we need to be concerned with.'

There is a near-war on in Kashmir and they are concerned with nuances. Better to nuke the bastards is my opinion, but not everyone agrees with me. They are all for nuanced relationships, which means that people get killed while we argue about whether to serve Rooh Afza or Real orange juice at the next summit. I suppose that is why Neeta joined the IFS, while I opted for the IAS. We roll up our sleeves and get to work, while they worry about nuances.

Sorry, but that was something I needed to get off my chest. We spend too much time around here splitting hairs anyway and nuances are the last thing we need.

Needless to say, I kept my feelings to myself. It makes for a more nuanced relationship with the external affairs lot. So:

'Point taken, Neeta. Now what's the problem?'

'That press conference.'

I was about to say that the Old Man was great, then realized I was repeating myself. The external affairs sorts repeat themselves only when there are nuances involved and I didn't need additional nuances cluttering up the conversation.

'Yes?'

'The Somali ambassador called. He was very upset.'

'About the Mogadishu bit? Come on, Neeta, you know as well as I do that Mogadishu is a shithole.'

'It is unpleasant, yes, but Somalia has longstanding fraternal relations with India. We are partners in the Non-Aligned Movement.'

The Non-Aligned Movement rarely moves. Not without the concurrence of the Russians anyway, but I kept that nuance to myself. 'Haven't they had a coup there?'

'Several, in fact. But they have consistently supported us in international fora. They are good friends and we need to mend the damage.'

'Why don't you tell the ambassador that it was all a joke? Tell him that we have shootouts in Delhi as well. That might make him feel a bit better.'

'It is not as simple as that.'

'You mean it is not nuanced enough?'

'I don't understand what you are saying.'

'Sorry, private joke.'

'Swami, this is a serious matter and not a time for levity.'

'Okay, what do you want me to do?'

'A statement from the PM...'

'No can do. A statement from the PM is a very serious matter. This doesn't qualify.'

'A personal apology to the ambassador, then, on behalf of the people of India.'

'Are you joking? Motwani will have my butt for even suggesting it. How about we ship some of our surplus wheat to Somalia? A gift from the people of India to their fraternal brothers and sisters in Somalia.'

'That will not work. They are a proud people. The ambassador is a proud man.'

'Come on, they are starving there.'

'That may well be the case. Under normal circumstances, a shipment would be welcomed. But not as a way of assuaging their hurt feelings.'

Assuaging their hurt feelings, my arse. Beggars can't be choosers, but like a good diplomat, I said nothing.

'How about a second row seat at the Republic Day parade?'

'Front row.'

'With the President and the Vice-President? Come off it, Neeta. Your Somali can nurse his hurt feelings till kingdom come. It is going to take a major geopolitical realignment before Somalia gets a front row seat at the parade. Tell you what. He can come around to 7 Race Course Drive and I'll ensure that the Old Man stops by and says hello.' An old trick the White House uses when someone inconvenient like the Dalai Lama comes calling.

'Swami, you don't get it, do you? Somalia is a Muslim country.'

'Oh dear! That had slipped my mind. You mean there might be another controversy about our treatment of certain communities.'

'The ambassador hinted at developments along those lines.'

'Son of a bitch!'

'I beg your pardon?'

'The guy has no right to be stirring up trouble in our country.'

'Perhaps, but what are you going to do about it? Dinner with the PM? A private dinner, of course.'

I hesitated. Dinner was invariably followed by the Choli Girl and her nude prancing. The Old Man preferred to eat dinner alone and it was usually a hurried affair. He would not enjoy the ambassador's company.

'Sorry. A private tea is the best I can do.'

'Menu?'

'Lassi, hot jalebis, samosas.'

'Add Rooh Afza and we have ourselves a deal.'

Our nuanced negotiations had just averted a diplomatic crisis.

3

The Sofa

1

The Old Man presided over what was called the Grand National Coalition (GNC). Some critics termed it the Go Nowhere Coalition. You couldn't blame the Old Man for this, though. Coalitions being coalitions, even the least significant constituent needed pampering. What this meant was that the cabinet consisted of a hundred and seventy-six members. Cabinet meetings were held in the Central Hall of Parliament as there was no other facility in Delhi both large enough and secure enough. Office space was scarce as well: some sixty ministers were told not to show up at their ministries and I was lucky to have an office to myself.

Then there was the Steering Body of the GNC. Only the Talkatora Stadium would accommodate this august body and the security arrangements needed to secure this facility were such that much of Delhi did without policemen when it met. Every attempt was made to keep the meeting dates a secret, generally without success. Each meeting, therefore, meant traffic mayhem and a rash of burglaries and murders.

This reflected ill on the government and the Old Man quite sensibly tried to keep the Steering Body meetings to a bare minimum. He did not always have his way.

'Oraonji,' he protested. 'We don't need a Steering Body meeting to discuss the cricket match.'

Laxman Oraon was the chairman of the Oraon People's Liberation Front of Jharkhand (L). His brother Ram was the chairman of the OPLFJ (R). Ram and Laxman were identical twins. Each was the only member of his party. Each claimed to be the 'real' OPLFJ. Each was a member of the cabinet and the Steering Body.

The Old Man couldn't tell one from the other.

'But Motwani sahib, what has happened is an insult to Jharkhand. The Steering Body has to be seized of the issue.'

'What issue? I thought you were calling about the cricket match.'

'Indeed, yes. The question is, why has Jharkhand not been allotted a cricket match? The BCCI is an upper caste conspiracy discriminating against the tribals of Jharkhand.'

'Then why don't you talk to the BCCI about it?'

'I have written three letters to them and they haven't replied.'

'Why don't you take it up with the minister of sports?'

'Motwani sahib, I am the minister of sports.'

'So sorry. All these cabinet reshuffles, you know. Plus I am an old man. Eighty-two years old. I remember the days when I was an assistant village munsif, fighting a guerrilla war against the British. Have I told you about how I was betrayed?'

'Motwani sahib, you have told us the story at every cabinet meeting.'

'I treated him like a brother. His sister was like a sister to me.' There was a pause. Memories of the sister were doubtless flooding his imagination. 'Yes, like a sister. I even let her tie me a rakhi one year. We were united in our cause. Who would have thought that...'

'Motwani sahib, I told you I have heard the story before. Now, about the Steering Body.'

'Why don't you forward a copy of the letter to my office? I'll make sure the BCCI sends you a reply.'

'The people of Jharkhand demand nothing less than a Steering Body meeting. The BCCI has insulted us. This is a matter of serious national importance. In fact, I shall be calling for the nationalization of the BCCI.'

'Oraonji, the days of nationalization are over.'

'This is a matter to be discussed by the Steering Body. I shall call for a committee to study the issue.'

'Oraonji, what do you really want?'

There was a long pause.

'Motwani sahib, can I sit with you and Mr Shah on the sofa at the test match? I am, after all, the minister for sports.'

'One day only.'

'Sahib, you have my full backing for whatever course of action you may choose to follow.'

'Thank you. I knew I could count on you.'

2

Seats on that sofa now became the most sought after prize in Delhi.

The Old Man had clearly misplayed his hand. The OPLFJ (L) was not about to be modest about its leader's achievement. A press conference was called to trumpet the fact. The OPLFJ (R) could not take this lying down. A spot on the sofa had to be found for Ram Oraon as well. That left a hundred and seventy-three ministers (the Old Man had an ex-officio spot on the sofa, remember) vying for eight sofa spots (four days, two spots per day). That left a hundred and sixty-five disappointed ministers who were potential troublemakers.

There were other claimants as well, including the Wakf Committee of the Bihar Assembly, a former deputy PM who had never won an election, a deep-voiced actor, and me. Someone, you see, had to be the Old Man's minder, making sure that he did not give Kashmir away in a fit of generosity. None of this group stood a chance in the face of the onslaught of the one hundred and seventy-three.

The Old Man, having created the mess, decided to fall ill and had himself admitted into hospital. The nation prayed for a weekday death so that they could have a holiday. As for me, I had to take on the wrath of the one hundred and seventy-three.

I was on the phone or in meetings all day, dealing with raised voices and raging tempers. At night, I had to lug the DVD player with the modified DVD to the hospital for the Old Man's edification. I prayed for his release – either from hospital or from this world.

Having one's hands on the levers of power is not all that it is cut out to be. Sleepless nights succeeded each other. I lost my sense of humour. I even yelled at Shah one day when he called to inquire after the Old Man's health and only narrowly averted a major diplomatic to-do. All my years of training and preparation for the job had come to naught. I had no idea how to break the logjam.

Inspiration struck when I least expected it. I was watching the scene in the Old Man's favourite film where everyone gathers together for a group portrait – and getting not a little distracted by the

Choli Girl – when it hit. Everyone wanted a seat on the sofa. Well, most of them would get it.

I ordered a special sofa that could seat twenty-four. It was very long, of course, and not everyone would be able to rub thighs with the PMs, but it ameliorated the extent of the problem. I could now accommodate a hundred and eight ministers (a hundred and ten including the Brothers Oraon) provided the match went into the fifth day. By having them exchange positions during each break, a good number could indulge in thigh-rubbing. That left only sixty-five troublemakers. Perhaps I could make sure these got offices somewhere in Delhi. Political crisis resolved. The Old Man would be pleased.

The GNC would live to see another day.

3

As I expected, the Old Man had himself discharged once I had solved his sofa problem.

Being eighty-two has its advantages. Aside from being able to pinch bottoms when he chooses, trips to the hospital arouse little comment or anxiety. Eighty-two-year-olds do get sick and tired every now and then and are not really expected to provide dynamic leadership to growing economies. The stock markets remained unperturbed, the rupee held its own, and life in general – except mine, of course – went on without losing a beat.

This general lack of interest in his well-being did not bother the Old Man at all. He was the PM, the rest of us billion odd Indians were not.

'Your health has improved, I hope.' It was Shah again.

'Ji haan, yes, you know how it is. Eighty-two years on this earth. Lots of wear and tear and all that.'

'I wanted to call you earlier, but heard you were in hospital.'

'Doctors' orders, no less. No visitors, no calls. Rest for the body, rest for the mind. Your father, he is also eighty, na?'

'Yes, yes, but I was not calling about my father.'

'You got those Indonesian nurses for him?'

'What? Oh, that. I've been busy. My father can wait. This is a serious matter.'

'What could be more serious than your father?'

'Keshavji, you are making fun of me.'

'Janaab, would I do such a thing to you?'

There were sounds not unlike those of someone keeping his feelings in check. 'Keshavji, your press conference.'

'Yes, yes. I clarified matters as you had requested – confirmed that I had indeed invited you. That was what you wanted, na?'

'You told them that I wanted to see *The Last Tango in Paris*.'

'Yes. You see, I have been told that it has been banned in this country. Lots of dirty, dirty things. Not suitable for Indians. But since you have requested it...'

'But I have *not* requested it!' Shah's voice had risen to a shout. 'What makes you think that... You know, that movie is un-Islamic. I don't watch such movies!'

'Then what movies do you watch?'

'What?'

'Janaab, you don't have to shout. I might be eighty-two years old, but I am not deaf. I asked you what movies you want to watch. Apart from *Last Tango*.'

'I told you I don't watch such movies!'

'Then why did you ask me to screen it for you?'

Another sound that I took to be that of teeth being gnashed. 'Okay, okay. There are other things I wish to discuss as well. But I want to be clear on one point. I do not want to see that movie. I don't see such movies.'

'How about *Kashmir Ki Kali*? Nice mountain scenery, pretty actress. Married a Muslim even.'

'Keshavji, I do not wish to discuss movies.'

'Oh. How disappointing!'

'What I do wish to discuss is another matter.'

'Yes, you've already told me that.'

'You said that I said that Fazlur Rehman wanted a transfer to Mogadishu.'

'Isn't that what you said?'

'No,' shouted Shah. 'That is not what I said.'

'Listen, why don't you call up Vikram Kapoor and tell him what you said? I need to go to the bathroom in a hurry. Doctors' orders. I am eighty-two years old, after all. Kapoor will pass on your message. I have to pass urine. Khuda hafiz.'

4

The IAS gets to work

1

Sardar Patel, the Iron Man of India, once described the IAS as the iron frame of India. I might be a mere cross-girder in the frame, but I know that I do my bit in keeping the structure of state from keeling over while the politicians and citizenry are off doing their thing.

The Old Man had dropped the Pakistani PM on our lap, so to speak, and it was for us to see that he didn't fall between the cracks (no pun intended).

We believed in the 'sound mind in a sound body' adage, and since good food was essential to the maintenance of sound bodies, I had the Taj cater our Executive Working Lunch. It was well appreciated.

'Swami,' said the cabinet secretary, 'that was an excellent lunch.'

'Thank you, sir.'

'Er... what was the cost?'

'For a hundred and twenty people, thirty-six thousand rupees, sir.'

'Er... the austerity drive the Old Man keeps talking about...'

'We were given a specific mandate to ensure that Shah's visit is a success.'

'Of course. Swami, I see you progressing far in the Service.'

'Thank you, sir.'

'Now,' continued the cabinet secretary. 'Down to business.'

There was a general clearing of throats and shuffling of papers. A sense of expectancy filled the air. The steel frame readied itself to do its job.

'We are gathered here,' said the cabinet secretary, 'at a moment when our great nation finds itself at a cusp, so to speak. Ahead lies a future whose outcome is in our hands. If we succeed, generations hence will thank us. Well, perhaps, the public in its ignorance of the hand that steers the nation's tiller might feel inclined to heap praise on the wrong heads. But we will not feel wronged. We chose to serve this great country not for praise or glory, for praise and glory are ephemeral and soon scattered by the shifting breezes, but for the satisfaction of seeing a job well done, for the satisfaction of knowing that the steps we have taken are steps towards a great and fulsome future when our country will once more live up to its promise of being the Land of Milk and Honey.'

Amen.

Actually, amen not so fast. The cabinet secretary had paused merely to sip a glass of Perrier. His sonorous voice had carried me along in its wake and it was only now when he paused that it occurred to me that the words were all too familiar. I crept up behind him.

'Sir?'

It didn't look like he had heard. 'Sir?' I spoke a little louder. The microphone picked up my voice and howled in agony. Annoyed, the cabinet secretary turned to stare at me.

'Can't you see that I haven't finished?' The mike howled once more and he hastily covered it.

'Sir, that speech.'

'What about it?'

'It is the PM's speech to the CII. I had sent you a copy for your approval before I passed it on to the PM. It must have got mixed up with the other papers.'

'Oh, um. How did that happen?'

'Could be Dixit, sir. He does get things mixed up sometimes.'

'Fixit' Dixit was a rival. I wasn't about to pass up on a chance to fix him.

'Bloody idiot! Embarrassing me like this. What is this meeting all about anyway?'

'The Pakistani PM's visit, sir.'

He shuffled through his pile of papers and extracted the relevant lot. 'Oh, here we are. I see. I see.'

The mike was uncovered once more.

'Technical difficulties, ladies and gentlemen, for which I apologize, but here we are. The visit of the Prime Minister of Pakistan. An important event, I need hardly reiterate. One that will keep us on our toes. Item 1. Hotel. Swami, can you elaborate?'

'Yes, sir. Thank you, sir. We need to decide which hotel the Prime Minister and his entourage will stay in.'

'Yes, indeed. Any suggestions?'

There were plenty of suggestions, followed by a lively discussion. The tourism ministry chaps wanted him to stay at the Ashok. They were trying to flog the place as part of a privatization binge and had found no takers. Too many roaches and rodents and far too many staff. The consultant's evaluation was all too succinct and had been shelved for fear of offending the said staff, roaches, rodents and the communist MPs. Now they thought that the Pakistani PM's visit would help pay for the exterminators (of roaches and rodents, not staff) whose services had been terminated earlier as per the government's Austerity Guidelines. But the external affairs lot cast their veto. No go – too many roaches and rodents.

The Taj Mansingh, the Maurya, the Oberoi all came in for discussion, but no consensus could be reached. It was finally decided that each hotel would be visited and various facilities, including restaurants and rooms, evaluated in detail. A committee of joint secretaries was formed to draw up a questionnaire that would be used for the evaluation. A committee of secretaries was formed to evaluate the facilities. They would report back a week after they received the questionnaire.

'Item 2. Visit to Itanagar and Tirunelveli.'

The discussion, if anything, was even livelier. The external affairs honchos wanted to accommodate the Pakistanis to the fullest extent possible. It was an important, even critical, visit and everything had to be done to make the visitors happy. The defence chaps were distinctly unhappy, Itanagar being a sensitive area and so on and so forth. The atomic energy chaps – a gloomy, taciturn, secretive lot – let it be known that Shah could not be allowed anywhere close to their precious reactor near Tirunelveli, friendly relations be damned. After all, national security issues were at stake. The defence and the AE chaps found common cause and stonewalled the issue.

The meeting threatened to end in chaos. I was forced to intervene and point out that no formal request had been received for the Itanagar and Tirunelveli legs of the trip. The issue could be postponed until the request was received. At that time, it could be pointed out that it was too late to make appropriate arrangements in those distant places. This calmed matters somewhat until someone, one of the defence chaps if I recall correctly, pointed out that no formal request had been received for the Shah visit in the first place. They suggested we adjourn the meeting until such time as a formal request was received.

The law ministry rep, silent all this while, piped up and said that in the opinion of his ministry, the visit, as defined thereto, was a private one and that in view of this, the use of government machinery vis-à-vis the visit was mala fide and prima facie illegal.

Utter chaos, with recriminations flung back and forth and so on. The external affairs honchos accused the defence chaps of being pedantic and bureaucratic in their approach and the law ministry of being anally retentive. No wonder they were asleep when the Pakistanis invaded Kargil. They were probably waiting for a formal declaration of war and the constitution of a committee to study the relevant articles under the Geneva Convention. The defence chaps gave as good as they got. The nuanced approach came in for considerable flak. Each side had ample ammunition at its disposal and used it. There is nothing so corrosive as inside knowledge of bureaucratic shenanigans. The steel frame was shaken to its foundations. Even I could do nothing about it. The buggers all had a point after all and I knew when to keep my trap shut. Items 3, 4, 5, 6, 7 and 8 would have to wait for another day. It was getting late and the cabinet secretary had a golf game waiting.

Our political masters would have to sort this out.

2

'What?' The Old Man was genuinely upset. I had just briefed him on the Executive Working Lunch.

'I'm sorry, sir, but in my opinion, these are matters to be decided by the cabinet. The Executive Working Group will not, in my opinion, reach a conclusion in time for the visit.'

'I am not asking for your opinion. I am asking for arrangements to be made for the visit. Next you will say that in your opinion, I have to call up the hotel and make all the arrangements myself. I am eighty-two years old with a weak heart and all. All your opinions are causing a big headache and my blood pressure to rise. In my opinion, you should all be transferred to Jhumritalayya and made to serve ten years RI.'

'Sir...'

'And you can take your bloody service rules with you and use it as toilet paper. Yes, I know what you are going to say. You cannot be transferred to Jhumritalayya as per your bloody service rules. Here I am trying to run a country, providing better life to a hundred crore Indians and here you are telling me that I have to be sitting at the bloody phone making hotel reservations for that idiot Shah. Enough of this nonsense! You can all go to hell. I am going to resign.'

'Sir...'

'No sir-ring business. Time for all that is past. You heard me. I am going to resign. You are reverting to your home state. Now go to hell.'

3

My home state, I'm sorry to say, is Bihar. Reverting to my home state meant milking Laloo's cows and serving Rabri's dal sabzi. Hell was a better proposition. A crisis, therefore, that was almost as threatening in its scope for the country as it was for me personally.

A crisis that mandated action.

Immediate action.

The first call was to the cabinet secretary. 'Swami speaking from the PMO, sir.'

'I am having an important personal meeting. Call me later.'

Sounded like the bar of the Golf Club. Important personal meeting, my arse.

'Sorry, sir, but there is a crisis.'

'What? Are the Pakistanis attacking?'

'No, sir. The Old Man is resigning.'

'Oh. That's no crisis.'

'The Executive Working Lunch, sir. You signed for it.'

'You mean, with the old man resigning....'

'Precisely, sir.'

'How much did you say it was?'

'Thirty-six thousand rupees, sir. I added a tip of four thousand on the assumption that...'

'Swami, this is a major crisis. I mean, I can't be expected to shell out forty thousand from my pocket. We need to do something about it.'

'Yes, sir.'

'We need to prevent the Old Man from resigning.'

'Yes, sir.'

'Any suggestions?'

'If you can get the President out of town, sir, there will be no one to accept the resignation. That would buy us some time.'

'Hmm. I'll see what can be done. Thank you, Swami. You are on the ball. Nice work.'

'Thank you, sir.'

4

Cabinet secretaries do not get to be cabinet secretaries by waiting for things to happen.

They make things happen.

They are the ones who get going when the going gets tough. Tough as nails, resourceful as a pack of foxes (yes, I know that foxes are solitary animals. I watch the National Geographic Channel. But a small factual inaccuracy is a minor matter when in service of an apt metaphor. After all, what is life without an apt metaphor or two), swift as a cheetah after its prey, the cabinet secretary is the formidable end product of a finely honed system of selection.

Ten minutes after our conversation, a helicopter lifted off from the Rashtrapati Bhawan helipad. Inside were the First Couple. They were on their way to Shimla to inaugurate a flower show. (The President, unlike the Old Man, was fond of Shimla. As a young man, he had been assigned the task of escorting the young Benazir Bhutto around Shimla. Whether the sparks that flew were mutual, one will never know, but ever since, he has been partial to strolls along the Mall with a faraway look in his eyes.)

Yes, I know that there are no flowers in Shimla in October. But arrangements had already been made for an executive jet to ferry flowers from Seville to Shimla. The flowers would be there when the President went to inaugurate the flower show the next day.

Expensive? Yes. But the Old Man had said that no expense was to be spared in making Shah's visit a success. And the Old Man, whether he liked it or not, was still the PM. And this little manoeuvre was a further step in ensuring the success of the visit.

5

We had bought ourselves time. Now we needed to change the Old Man's mind. That forty thousand rupee bill hung like the Sword of Damocles over our heads and we knew that we could brook no failure in the task we had set ourselves.

The Old Man wouldn't make things easy for us. As an eighty-two year old with a lifetime of politics under his belt, he knew all about resignation dramas and the need to draw them out to satisfactory conclusions. Caesar spurned the throne thrice, but that was two millennia ago. Expectations had progressed since then along with politicians' ability to count past three.

Besides, there was this lurking fear that the Old Man really meant it this time.

The first skirmishes were straight from the Politician's Handbook. The defence minister and the law minister called on the Old Man, apologized for the presumption of their nominees to the Executive Working Lunch, assured him of their support in this and all other matters, and called on him to rethink his decision.

The Old Man sat sphinx-like through all this, breaking his silence only to offer the obligatory chai and biscuits. It was a most impressive performance.

Defence and Law were followed by their colleagues. Given the numbers involved, I had to schedule appointments at fifteen minute intervals. Politics is all about gestures. Each minister insisted on draping a shawl over the Old Man. In turn, I had to keep track of ministerial biscuit and drink preferences.

Matching ministers with biscuits, tea, soft drinks and the like required logistical planning of a high order. Making sure each minister left when his time was up required political gestures of a high order. Making sure they didn't meet each other on their way in and out required split second timing of a high order. This last was particularly important as these were supposed to be spontaneous expressions of support and they didn't expect to find themselves tripping over each other in the corridors of 7 Race Course Road.

Before each of the one hundred and seventy-six made his or her way into the sanctum sanctorum, I needed to brief the Old Man. I've already alluded to his tendency to mistake one minister for another. This was pardonable in normal times, but not in these politically fraught ones, when a single misstep could result in a national crisis.

It took a week to clear the backlog.

Keeping track of ministers, ministerial details, schedules, biscuits, Rooh Afza and the rest was a nerve-wracking business. There were a hundred things that could have gone wrong, any one of which would have spelt disaster. That nothing went wrong was a tribute to my abilities under extreme stress. A lesser man might have caved in under the pressure and lost his nerve. I kept mine. It was in many ways my finest hour, but I must admit it took its toll. I was, to put not too fine a point on it, a wreck at the end of it.

The Old Man, on the other hand, enjoyed every minute of it. The politician in him was in his element. The fawning sidekicks, the false flattery, the utterly insincere words of devotion and support, he saw humour in all this. He revelled in their discomfiture. For the moment at least, he, and only he, mattered. He was the shameless manipulator of sentiments and events – the nation was in thrall to him.

As if my daily labours were not enough, he insisted on his nightly dose of the Choli Girl and his pleasure at the nightly rump show was genuine and uninhibited.

A week had gone by and what had we achieved? Nothing. Yes, nothing. In some ways, I had overlooked the forest for the trees. In keeping track of a hundred minute details, I had forgotten the overarching purpose of it all – the retraction of the resignation.

The cabinet secretary had done his part. Shimla over and done with, he had unearthed some half-forgotten invitations from minor African countries. Rashtrapatiji and wife were off enjoying traditional tribal dances in the sun swept savannah.

Prevented from submitting his resignation, the Old Man nonetheless refused to retract it. Exhausted from a week of resignation drama management, I ventured to ask him if he had considered changing his mind.

He smiled a wicked smile. 'Swami, I know that Jhumritalayya is in Jharkhand now. But you are afraid of going to Patna, na? That is why this great anxiety about my resignation.'

'No, sir. I have devoted my life to the service of the country. It matters not whether I serve it here or in Patna. I am concerned only about the country. The country needs you at its helm, sir.'

'You are a bad liar, Swami.'

'You are doing me a disservice, sir. My concern is genuine.'

'Your concern is genuine? You want me to get BP dealing with those... those... how many of those clowns are there anyway?'

'A hundred and seventy-six, sir.'

'A hundred and seventy-six? Let someone else deal with them. I am fed up of them. They have all licked my arse, now I can kick their arses. Nothing would give me greater pleasure. Better still, dissolve the Parliament. Let them waste their money getting elected. Serve them right, after all the headaches they have given me.'

'You can't do this, sir.'

'Why not?'

'Sir, Mr Shah's visit. If you dissolve Parliament now... surely he cannot visit as the guest of a caretaker government. There will be a significant diplomatic fallout. It would be unwise at this time.'

'Swami, you are a bureaucrat, you give bureaucratic advice. Me, I want to settle down in Rishikesh. Bathe in the Holy Ganga, meditate.'

'Sir, there is no alcohol served in Rishikesh.'

'I am giving up alcohol. If Valmiki could give up sin, I can give up alcohol.'

'But...'

'No buts. When Rashtrapatiji returns, I am resigning. Decision final.'

6

It was a bleak prospect and the bleakness of it overwhelmed me. I looked around my office – at the drapes I had ordered when I moved in, at the leather and steel sofa set, at the carpet that had been smuggled in from Iran, at the Wilton carpet that lay on top of it, at the air-conditioning system that had been upgraded just prior to the previous summer, at my new Apple Macbook Air, and the expansive view across the lawns of 7 Race Course Drive. All this and the knowledge that I was witness to the cut and thrust of politics, to the ebb and flow of decisions that marked out the path India would follow in the years, even generations, to come. I had ascended rarefied heights and, now, as I peered into the abyss that yawned before me, all I could see was a humdrum existence – a dusty office somewhere in Patna, a rickety old Ambassador to take me to and from work, a job administering the animal husbandry department or some such.

Worthy work, perhaps, but unworthy of someone with my world view and experience.

The phone rang. I let it ring. The fax machine in the corner chattered into life and spewed out reams of paper. I let the coils of paper accumulate on the floor. I felt tears start up in my eyes. My thoughts jammed, froze. I then did what I should have done much earlier. I took out the picture of Parthasarathy Swami from my desk drawer, propped it up in front of me and prayed – prayed hard and with the utmost sincerity.

The Lord listened to me as I knew He would.

7

One nice thing about the IAS is that brother (and sister) officers are always ready to help with titbits of information. The fact that I am the PM's personal secretary helps, of course, as does the fact that their transfer and promotion files go through my office. I do like to think, though, that camaraderie and esprit de corps play a part. Together we constitute the iron frame and each one of us, from the tiniest screw to the mightiest of girders, works in harmony to keep the structure standing.

A few phone calls and some discreet questions later, I learned the following:

1. That the Old Man had obtained spiritual guidance from one Paramacharya Sri Sri Sri Ramananda Swami.
2. That the said Paramacharya had an ashram in Rishikesh.
3. That the said ashram had been constructed on government-owned land.
4. That no application had been made for permission to construct the said ashram.
5. That additional structures – a seven-storey residential complex and a domed meditation hall – were currently under construction.
6. That the said Paramacharya was attempting to get the government to divert the Ganga with the aim of reclaiming some additional land for the said ashram.

8

Paramacharya Sri Sri Sri Ramananda Swami proved to be inaccessible to the general public. I had hoped to approach him discreetly, but found this impossible. The ashram was a thriving enterprise, though I couldn't imagine how any meditation could go on amidst the racket created by all the construction equipment. There were officials, senior officials and very senior officials.

My first approach, as a salvation-seeking member of the public, came up short. A novitiate in his early twenties was all that could be spared for my needs.

The Paramacharya? The novitiate's eyes bulged in disbelief. He hadn't met the Paramacharya either and he had been there four years. Who got to meet the great man, then? God, certainly, but beyond that he couldn't say. In fact, he had yet to meet anyone who had met the Paramacharya.

There was nothing to do but pull rank.

I was wafted up the hierarchy. Officials took me up to senior officials. They, in turn, took me up to very senior officials. I was made to wait a bit before being ushered into a large office. It didn't look all that different from mine, but the construction definitely took away from the view.

There was a doorway leading to what must have been the sanctum sanctorum and the Paramacharya entered through this. He was a bit nonplussed when I made to shake his hands, but recovered quickly. I suppose he was used to people prostrating themselves before him, but then I suppose he hadn't met too many senior IAS officers either.

He was much younger than I had expected, not much more than forty. He sported the obligatory beard and long hair and was extraordinarily handsome. His shoulders and exposed arms were well muscled.

An acolyte brought in two glasses of rose tinted water. 'No intoxicants here, Mr Swami,' he said. 'I believe it gets in the way of a meaningful realization of the Almighty.' He spoke in a clear, well-accented voice.

'How many years have you been here?' I asked.

'Seven,' he replied. 'I came here after fifteen years of wandering in the far reaches of the Himalayas.'

'You don't look very old.'

'I am older than you think. Realization of the Almighty can do this to the body.'

I was impressed.

'Mr Swami, I take it you are here in connection with Mr Motwani's impending move here.'

'Well, yes. Has he been planning this for a long time?' I needed to know just how serious the Old Man was.

'He has been talking about it in general terms for some time, but his plans took concrete shape only very recently.'

'The week before last?'

'That seems about right. Now how can I help you?'

What was I to say? Here was someone who had realized the Almighty and here I was trying to cut a deal. Then I remembered that the land we were on was government land, that there was talk of diverting the river. The Paramacharya must know the ways of the world.

I tried the direct approach:

'Look, the nation needs Mr Motwani's services. You must persuade him to postpone his plans.'

The Paramacharya looked puzzled. 'I don't understand. There can be nothing more fulfilling for a man than attaining sanyas in Rishikesh. We encourage all our followers to consider settling here after their retirement and, in our modest way, take them along the path of realization. Telling someone not to come here goes against everything we stand for.'

'I am not asking you to cancel his plans, merely to postpone them for a year, or two, or three.'

'Mr Motwani is in the autumn of his life. What you are suggesting is inappropriate, and particularly inappropriate for someone like Mr Motwani.'

Why was he making it so difficult? I was hoping not to get into the messy details of the quid pro quo, but he was leaving me no alternative.

'Look, if Motwani comes here as planned, I'll make sure every newspaper knows that you are building on government land. I'll also make sure everyone knows about the plan to divert the river. Damn it, I'll make sure that Baba Amte and Medha Patkar and Arundhati Roy and the rest all set up camps here in protest.'

I must say he took it without flinching. Perhaps realizing the Almighty does that to you. When he spoke, it was in the same even tone of voice.

'Having Mr Motwani here is important to me personally and to the ashram.'

Aha! He was bargaining now.

'All I'm asking for is a postponement.'

'A year is a long time in the life of an eighty-two year old man.'

'Six months. You pick an auspicious date.'

'Three months and we can shake hands.'

'He has to withdraw his resignation, not merely postpone it.'

'He withdraws his resignation, but quits three months later.'

Actually, a month was all I was looking for, but I made a big show of pursing my lips, looking meaningfully out of the window and tapping my feet before allowing my hand to be shaken.

'I take it the construction can go on?'

He was making sure there was no misunderstanding about the fine print.

'Yes, and I don't care how the Ganga flows into the sea as long as it continues to flow into the sea.'

5

Personal Problems

1

Shah's visit was drawing nigh. Various working groups had been constituted to go into the modalities of the visit. There was the odd grumble or two from the law ministry about the legality of the whole thing, but they kept their mutterings to the darker corners of the ministry. A security blanket was being thrown around the city and this meant the usual round of disruptions for the citizenry.

2

'Swami!'

'Yes, sir?'

'Shah called and brought up a couple of things.'

'I'm sorry, sir, but are you saying that a telephone call from Mr Shah came through without my being aware of it?'

'Why should you be aware of it?'

'I am your PA, sir, and would like to make sure you are not disturbed by any unnecessary phone calls.'

'You are saying that Shah's call is an unnecessary one?'

'No, not at all, sir. It is just that...'

'You go to the bathroom at eleven every morning. That's when Shah called. You see, neither he nor I want you listening in on our private conversations. Bad manners. I'm surprised they didn't teach you all that at the Mussoorie Academy. Maybe I should constitute a committee, a Standing Committee of Parliament maybe, to go into the syllabus at the academy and other matters. You can testify before the committee. Then I can receive my phone calls in peace.'

I was shaken and indignant.

'I am upset at your insinuations, sir. I am upset that you have thought fit to keep track of my private habits.'

'Arre, I have better things to do. The ISI found out. Shah told me.'

'The ISI – and what else did they find out?'

'That you have piles. I know a good fellow in Paharganj. Very discreet. Will take care of your piles without an operation. Herbal treatment. Then you can take a week off in Rishikesh to recover. I'll arrange with Guruji to get an AC room for you.'

'Sir...'

'As I was saying, Shah brought up a couple of things.'

'I DO NOT HAVE PILES!' I said as forcefully as I could, given that I was talking to the PM.

'Not piles? Then something else in your bum. You see, the ISI gets a few details wrong now and then. Like my watching Amitabh Bachchan movies. Have you seen *Don*?'

'Yes, but...'

'I think I will show it to Shah. He will enjoy it.'

'There is nothing wrong with my bum.'

'There must be. Even the CIA are talking about it.'

'The CIA? What have they got to do with this, sir?'

'I don't know. But the other day, the US ambassador was saying that – how do you say it? – that you were anal retentive. See, I even wrote it down so I wouldn't forget it. You take this to that fellow in Paharganj. I'll promise not to tell anyone, even the ISI and the CIA.'

I was speechless with rage and spoke only with difficulty. I was aiming for the tone of voice generally described as dripping with sarcasm, but, in my general agitation, might well have sounded very different.

'I take it, sir, that the US ambassador chose to call when I was otherwise occupied.'

'Yes, yes. He also called when you were in the bathroom. It seems the ISI and the CIA have exchanged information on these matters.'

'And who else, if I may ask, called when I was otherwise occupied?'

'I don't keep a list. But recently, lots of people have been calling when you were in the loo. I think the Mossad also knows about it because the Israeli PM called.'

'Sir, I cannot abide this very casual dismissal of my dignity. I have striven to serve and assist you to the best of my abilities. I have broken my back, sweated blood, endured long nights without sleep – all to help you in the performance of your duties. Serving my country and serving you have been the only touchstones I have lived by. I am sorry that these efforts have been insufficiently recognized. I have craved no reward other than the satisfaction of having my work appreciated. Even this meagre reward has been denied me. It has been my privilege to have served you, but it is now time for me to go. I am submitting my resignation, sir, and request you to accept it with the utmost celerity.'

'Don't be a fool, Swami. Everybody knowing your bathroom time is no reason to resign.'

'My decision is final, sir.'

'Very well, then. I shall have to discuss this proposal for a game of buzkashi with someone else.'

3

The days dragged by.

'Fixit' Dixit, that incompetent fool, had taken my place. I had expected a few calls – of commiseration, requests to withdraw my resignation, offers of alternative postings. None were forthcoming. The phone sat silently and I waited in futile silence beside it.

The days dragged by and brought with them feelings of anger, of inadequacy, of impotence. Surely someone must have noticed my absence? I knew that this wasn't a sentimental town, and sentiment was not what I was looking for. I did expect the odd word of appreciation, a quiet word or two of thanks, commiseration at having come to grief at the hands of a two-bit politician, a few words of empathy – in other words, the suggestion that mine was a sacrifice made for a cause.

No such luck.

The country stumbled on towards an uncertain destiny and I was left forgotten on the wayside.

Not entirely forgotten.

From deep within the bowels of government came a missive demanding that I surrender my phone and another demanding that I vacate my quarters forthwith. Signed by low-level twits whose penmanship left everything to be desired. Twits who, mere days earlier, would have been grovelling at my feet.

The silence I could deal with. These gratuitous insults I could not ignore. I swallowed my pride and picked up the phone. I tried the Old Man and found myself speaking to Dixit. He couldn't keep the smirk out of his voice as he told me that the Old Man was busy with the Pakistani PM's Visit and therefore unavailable for discussions. I couldn't very well ask old Fixit to look into my phone and house problem. It would be demeaning at best and, more likely than not, invite a snub.

I tried the cabinet secretary. Busy with the Visit.

I tried the foreign secretary. Busy with the Visit.

Ditto the home secretary, the law secretary, the defence secretary, the secretary for company affairs, the secretary for social uplift, the secretary for Harijan welfare and the secretary for animal husbandry.

In desperation, I even tried Neeta.

You guessed it – Busy with the Visit.

All of Delhi was Busy with the Visit and here I was, friendless and facing the threat of eviction and the loss of my phone. Even my batman knew which way the wind was blowing. He told me one morning that he had secured a transfer to Railway Bhawan and that I would henceforth have to make my own idlis.

The days dragged by.

4

All Delhi was agog with the Visit.

Shah to Visit Dilli Haat
By Our Correspondent

As the Prime Minister of Pakistan's
visit draws nigh, the government is
sparing no effort to ensure that the
visit is a success. The hiccups,
misunderstandings and the harsh
words which followed the initial
announcements are now ascribed to
bureaucratic inertia and bungling. An
atmosphere of bonhomie now prevails.
Mr Anirudh Dixit, IAS, the personal
secretary to the Prime Minister, who
was brought in with an explicit mandate
to smooth things over, is coordinating
all aspects of the visit from a
specially-equipped office functioning
within the PMO.

At a briefing for selected journalists,
Mr Dixit described how the logistics
and security aspects of the visit were
being coordinated from his office.

'Mr Shah's visit is an important one.
The Prime Minister has repeatedly
emphasized his desire that the visit
leave a lasting impression of India's
friendly intentions towards Pakistan.
My office is leaving no stone unturned

to meet his expectations,' said Mr Dixit.

While the test match remains the highlight of the visit, a number of other events have been added to Mr Shah's itinerary. The idea, said Mr Dixit, was to showcase various aspects of Indian history, society and culture.

Mr Dixit revealed that an informal evening at the Dilli Haat was on the cards. After a performance by traditional puppeteers, a meal catered by chefs from the Sikkim, Bengal and Tamil Nadu stalls would serve to highlight the varied cuisine of India. Other such evenings are being planned and the details will be announced in due course.

The scale of planning for what is in reality a private visit is unprecedented. It may be recalled that the late General Zia ul Haq visited India in the 1980s to witness a cricket match. At that time, General Haq flew in and out on the same day and an air of informality prevailed. It says much for the importance this government places on relations with its neighbour that the arrangements rival that of an important state visit.

Fixit was certainly one for getting his name in the news. I had preferred to work behind the scenes, getting pleasure and satisfaction from a job well done or a crisis deftly averted, rather than this shameless self-promotion.

Then there was this completely unnecessary denigration of the work I had done.

Bureaucratic inertia and bungling, my foot! Blame Vikram Kapoor and the IFS for that.

The least Dixit could have done was give me credit for averting major crises even as the visit threatened to go off the rails. I was glad when this exercise in puffery and self-aggrandization got its due reward.

5

Controversy over Dilli Haat Visit
By Our Correspondent

The proposed visit to Dilli Haat by the visiting Pakistani dignitaries has aroused strong feelings from an unexpected quarter.

It may be recalled that Mr Anirudh Dixit, IAS, the personal secretary to the Prime Minister, had arranged an evening at Dilli Haat for the Pakistanis. A puppet show was to be followed by a meal catered by Sikkimese, Bengali and Tamilian chefs.

The chief minister of Gujarat yesterday expressed shock at the exclusion of Gujarati cuisine from the proposed menu.

'Gujarat is the home of Mahatma Gandhi, the Father of India. What better tribute to his ideals than to serve the VIP visitors food from his home state?' asked Mr Makhanbhai Patel, chief minister of Gujarat. 'The people of Gujarat are upset and disappointed that Gujarati food has been overlooked. We appeal to the Prime Minister to rectify this oversight.'

When asked what action he would take if his appeal was ignored, Mr Patel said that he would follow the Mahatma's example and begin an indefinite fast until his demand was met. 'It is a matter of honour for Gujaratis,' said Mr Patel. 'I shall begin my fast tomorrow.'

Neither Mr Dixit nor the Prime Minister were available for comment.

There was more to follow:

Dilli Haat Controversy Snowballs
By Our Special Correspondent

The row over the menu for the Pakistani delegation's dinner at Dilli Haat threatened to go out of control.

As was reported yesterday, the chief minister of Gujarat began an indefinite fast to protest the exclusion of Gujarati food from the menu.

Further protests regarding the same issue erupted across the country.

In Kerala, the chief minister, Mr Baby Jesus, expressed regret that traditional Keralite dishes like avial, idiappam and karimeen pozhichattu had been excluded. 'What sort of picture of our country will Mr Shah and his group form? Kerala is God's Own Country. How could the Prime Minister ignore us?' Mr Jesus demurred when asked if he would join Mr Patel in an indefinite fast. 'We have yet to decide our course of action,' he said. 'We will have an all party meet to decide our course of action. In the meanwhile, I will strongly protest to the Prime Minister.'

In Nagaland, the chief minister, Mr Lowang Dang Wang, was aghast that Sikkimese food had gained precedence over Naga food. 'This is our reward for being part of India since 1947. Sikkim joined only in 1975. Yet, their food has gained precedence over ours. How can I face my people when the Centre chooses to treat us so shabbily? How can I resist calls for independence when the Centre is so indifferent to the aspirations of the Naga people?'

In Karnataka, the chief minister, Mr Chikkaveeraraja, complained that the Centre was favouring Tamil Nadu. 'In all matters, be it Cauvery water or food, the Centre is playing favourites.

Now the Pakistani visitors are being denied bisi bele bath, maddur vadai and other Kannadiga delicacies. I shall be protesting strongly against this.'

In Tamil Nadu, three people in Kumbakonam committed self-immolation on hearing Mr Chikkaveeraraja's comments. One person succumbed to his injuries and the other two are stated to be in a critical condition. The chief minister announced an ex-gratia payment for the deceased and appealed for calm. In response to a question, he stated, 'I shall endeavour to ensure that Tamil food remains on the menu.'

In Chandigarh, the chief minister of Punjab, Mr Satnam Singh Bhains, added to the clamour, saying, 'Mr Shah is a Punjab da puttar. Denying him Punjabi food is like denying a calf milk. This is a deliberate insult to Punjab and Punjabis. There shall be a statewide bandh tomorrow in protest.' There were unconfirmed reports that effigies of the Prime Minister were burned in Jalandhar, Amritsar and Tarn Taran.

As the row over the Dilli Haat menu engulfed the country, neither the PM nor his personal secretary, Mr Anirudh Dixit, were available for comment.

6

Interesting.

Now Shah, who must have been watching the goings-on with glee, decided to fan the flames.

Pak PM Calls for Breakup of India
By Our Special Correspondent

Reacting to the fracas in India about the proposed menu for his dinner at Dilli Haat, the Prime Minister of Pakistan offered to incorporate any dissatisfied Indian state into a Greater Pakistan. 'There seems to be a lot of dissatisfaction in India. People from differing parts of the country are questioning the Centre. Here in Pakistan, we treat all states equally. So, they are welcome to join us.'

Asked about the problems arising from Hindu or Christian majority states joining an Islamic Pakistan, he said that 'this only proves that we are Islamic but secular'. Replying to a question about his preferred diet, he said that he 'preferred Punjabi food. If Indian Punjab is unhappy about this matter, a unified Punjab in Pakistan is the dream of all Punjabis.'

Responding to Mr Shah's comments, the foreign affairs ministry in New Delhi had this reaction: 'We deplore the insinuations of the Prime Minister of Pakistan. The territorial integrity of India is inviolable. The mischievous suggestions put forth by the Prime Minister of Pakistan deserve our unreserved contempt. We refuse to be drawn further into this pointless discussion.'

In this overheated atmosphere, it is unclear whether Mr Shah's proposed visit to Delhi will go ahead. Neither the PM nor his personal secretary, Mr Anirudh Dixit, were available for comment on this latest development.

I knew that I was home free. It was just a matter of time, and when the call came, I put on my most injured air.

'Swami?'

'Yes, sir.'

'This is the PM speaking.'

'Yes, sir.'

'Have you been reading the papers?'

'The home ministry has cut off my supply of papers, sir.'

'What? Can't you go and buy a paper? Don't you watch TV?'

'I have received an eviction notice, as also a notice warning me that my telephone is to be disconnected. I have been running from pillar to post trying to get a deferment. I haven't had time to buy a newspaper.'

'Why didn't you call me?'

'I did, sir. Dixit wouldn't let me speak to you. He said that you were very busy.'

'Dixit? Dixit? That Dixit had no business doing that. Do you know what that Dixit has gone and done?'

'No, sir.'

'He has created a bloody mess.'

'I'm not surprised, sir.'

'What? What did you say?'

'I said that I'm not surprised that Dixit has failed to meet your expectations as far as the discharge of his duties is concerned.'

'Then who sent him here?'

'The question should be addressed to the cabinet secretary, sir.'

'What should I do about him?'

'I cannot presume to advise you about the course of action to be taken with such a senior officer, sir.'

'I mean Dixit, for heaven's sake.'

'As one who is no longer in service, I cannot presume to render advice...'

'Arre, ullu ke patthe! Don't you understand? I want you back here. I should never have let you go. But where do I post this Dixit?'

'Commercial attaché in Mogadishu might be an appropriate posting for someone with his talents, sir.'

6

Dousing the Fires

1

It had, I must admit, been an unnerving experience. It had also been a learning experience. I knew where I stood, whom I could count on (no one), and what really mattered in my life (myself). A streak of cynicism had permeated my being, what idealism there had been had been sent packing. I saw the world in a cold harsh light. My sense of right and wrong had blurred into an evaluation of possibilities.

I could, I suppose, have spent days gnashing my teeth about the whole blasted thing, but there was work to do, fires to put out, not least the one Dixit had unleashed on the Indian polity.

Fire-fighters have evolved a technique for controlling wildfires. This involves setting off a counter blaze that stops the original conflagration in its tracks. Homoeopaths have developed similar techniques: they use small doses of poison to counter ailments. What I decided on was an amalgam of these approaches.

Cricket fever, Visit fever and Menu fever had all reached a high pitch and, when I invited a few journalists for a chat, there were a hundred others clamouring for an invite. I counselled patience – I had use for them, too.

'There has been much said about what is to be served to the visiting Pakistanis. I would like to clarify that, as a secular country, we respect the religious sentiments of the Muslims and that under no circumstances will we serve pork chops to the visiting dignitaries.'

There was a moment's stunned silence before the bedlam of questions hit me.

'Mr Swami, why this denial?'

'I want to make our position crystal clear.'

'Was there a suggestion that pork chops be served?'

'We had not given any thought to it.'

'Was there a request from any of the Pakistanis?'

'I'm sorry. I cannot comment on that.'

'You mean that they *asked* you to serve pork chops?'

'I said that I cannot comment on that.'

'Was there any suggestion from their side that liquor be served at any of the dinners?'

'In keeping with the example set by Mahatma Gandhi, we do not serve liquor at state banquets.'

'Was there a request for liquor at any of the informal dinners?'

'I cannot comment on that.'

2

Note that I had said nothing.

Insinuation, though, has its uses.

The suggestion took fire as I had anticipated. Shah and his minions spent the next three days denying the pork chops and liquor stories. It certainly did not help Shah's cause that he had been a bon vivant in his youth and that his denials did not entirely ring true. An enterprising Pakistani journalist somehow unearthed an old English girlfriend of Shah and she had plenty to say. She had been unceremoniously dumped after three years of providing him bacon and sausages for breakfast and happy for the chance to get her own back.

Assorted mullahs got into the act and Shah was forced to assert and reassert his Islamic credentials.

As anticipated, the Dilli Haat story lost its relevance. Makhanbhai Patel quietly dropped his indefinite fast, sensing which way the wind was blowing. Bhains dropped his plans for a bandh. Chikkaveeraraja, Baby Jesus and the rest, with their finely-honed political instincts, decided that food was not worth their political while and moved on to other things.

Round one to us.

Time, then, for Round Two.

I called in the journalists who had been left out earlier. There was some general chitchat before I let slip the buzkashi suggestion.

Time was when the average Indian journalist could have held his own on the finer points of the game. This lot – as I had anticipated – had no idea what it was. Time, once more, to plant a suggestion or two.

It was, I told them, a barbaric Afghan game involving the head of a newly-slaughtered cow. Given Indian sensibilities about cows, it was a most insensitive proposal. Naturally, we were appalled at the idea and had turned it down post-haste.

Besides, the Pakistanis had still not got back to us about the tennis match.

The headlines the next day were suitably lurid:

'Pak PM Insults Hindus'
'Pak PM Insults All of India'
'Animal Rights Activists Denounce Pak PM'
'No Tennis. Let's Kill Cows Instead, Says Shah.'
'Indian Dignity versus Pak Bloodthirstiness'

3

Shah was on the phone first thing next morning.

'I'm sorry sir, but the PM is still asleep,' I told him.

'Wake him up. This is urgent.'

'What may I tell him is the matter, sir?'

'This is life and death. Call him immediately.'

'Are you declaring war on us, sir?'

'Of course, not.'

'In that case, he is not to be woken up. You see, sir, he is eighty-two years old and under doctor's orders to get a good night's sleep.'

'This is important, I am telling you,' he shouted.

I continued as if he hadn't spoken. 'Given the doctor's orders, the National Security Council determined that the PM would be woken up only in case of an emergency. An emergency was then defined as a declaration of war by an enemy country. The Emergency Procedures Document is clear on this point.'

'Goddammit, what do I have to do to wake him up?'

'Declare war, sir.'

'But... but...'

'I assure you, sir, that I shall inform Mr Motwani about your call at the earliest. What might I tell him is the reason for this call?'

'Haven't you read the papers?'

'Yes, sir.'

'Then you bloody well know what this is about.'

'Have you got permission from your generals for the tennis match, sir?'

'You goddamned nincompoop!'

'I think you should be aware that this conversation is being taped, sir.' It wasn't, but there's little harm in the odd white lie.

'You... you... you...'

'There would be a diplomatic fracas if the news of your use of intemperate language towards a bureaucrat of another country became public.'

There were some odd noises, reminiscent of a pressure cooker letting off steam. 'Okay, okay. I just want to make it perfectly clear that there is no proposal from our side for a game of buzkashi.'

'Would you care to repeat that, sir?'

'There is no proposal from our side for a game of buzkashi.'

'Thank you, sir. I will pass on the message to the PM. About the taped conversation...'

'Yes?'

'Sorry, but I was just pulling your leg. We Indians have a sense of humour, you know...'

'You cheeky son of a swine! Why did Keshavji bring you back? Just when we had figured a way to get you out of the loop.'

'For the record, sir, you can inform the ISI that I've changed my bathroom timings.'

'What are you talking about?'

'About calling when I was not available to introduce the caller to the PM.'

'What is all this about the ISI and the bathroom? Your PM sent a diplomatic note, asking me to call at eleven in the morning.'

'I beg your pardon, sir?'

'Are you deaf? Your PM asked me to call at eleven. I don't know what this has to do with the ISI and the bathroom. If you ask me, you are all paranoid about the ISI. And you, when I do talk to your PM, I'll be sure to tell him about your unacceptable cheekiness.'

Hell hath no fury like a PM scorned. I put aside my feelings at the Old Man's perfidy and hastened to cover my butt.

4

Pak PM Climbs Down on Buzkashi Proposal
By Our Special Correspondent

The Prime Minister of Pakistan has withdrawn his proposal for the game of buzkashi, which was to be held during his visit to India. Sources indicate that Mr Shah was shaken at the feelings his proposal had aroused. He apologized to the People of India for putting forward the suggestion without giving due regard to the sensitivities involved. He also clarified that the game involved a goat and not a cow. The Indian Prime Minister accepted the apologies on behalf of the People of India.

Only after I had fed this to the press did I tell the Old Man about Shah's call. I thought it prudent to avoid mention of the ISI and the bathroom and tried to emphasize the positive – how I had got Shah to back down and how I had made it appear that he had eaten crow.

Politics is all about ends justifying means and I was sure the Old Man would appreciate this. Besides, he had no alternative. Fixit Dixit had already sent in a requisition for some bulletproof glass for his windows and looked well ensconced in Mogadishu.

I have to say that I trod on eggshells the next few days. The Old Man gave me peculiar looks, but said nothing. Nothing, that is, apart from the usual give-and-take between the PM and his secretary. What transpired between Shah and the Old Man stayed secret. In view of the sensibilities involved, I had not listened in, and could only wonder at the diplomatic hoops the two must have jumped through.

7

Cultural Matters

1

Things were progressing apace on other fronts.

The Song and Dance Division of the ministry of information and broadcasting wanted to, you guessed it, make a song and dance about the Pakistani PM's visit. Time was when the sods had more than enough to do. Along with the Films Division, they took very seriously their self-appointed task of entertaining the movie going masses with songs and dances before the real entertainment – songs and dances of less than folkloric provenance – got under way.

Reforms, cable and satellite TV and the unhealthy influence of American mass culture all meant reduced budgets and vastly reduced (read, non-existent) audiences. The flower that was socialist India's contribution to culture had withered away. The creative geniuses behind it now spent their time drinking tea, enjoying the winter sunshine and agitating for a return to more halcyon days.

But here, they sensed an opportunity.

I suspect Dixit's daft suggestion about an ethnic dinner at Dilli Haat had given them ideas and now Sudhendu Ranjan Mohanty, IAS, sat before me with an equally daft suggestion.

'You see,' he said, peering at me through horn-rimmed spectacles. 'The Pakistani PM should be introduced to the beauty and variety of Indian culture.'

'He has already seen all the Amitabh Bachchan movies.'

'You are not paying sufficient attention. I said Indian culture, not Indian movies.'

'All the same, yaar.'

'No, no, no! I strongly resent the insinuation.'

I was busy, I had a hundred important details to take care of, and here he was, strongly resenting the insinuation. The blighter ought to have realized that the only reason he was sitting in my sanctum sanctorum in the first place was that he was a brother IAS officer. A nut or a screw in the general scheme of things, but an IAS officer for all that – and entitled to the courtesies that a brother officer extends to another. This, though, was carrying things too far. Resenting the insinuation, my arse.

I put on my coldest voice and stared meaningfully at the stacks of paper on my desk. 'Is that so? Then what do you suggest?'

'A variety programme highlighting the various aspects of Indian culture.'

'India has twenty-seven states. Do you propose to include a sample from each one in this variety programme of yours?'

'No, no, not at all. A sample. For example, a Odissi dance to showcase Indian dance.'

Trust an Oriya to showcase Odissi. He probably didn't even know superior dance forms such as Bharatanatyam existed.

'Sorry, that will not do.'

'But why?'

'Any such programme must include items from all states. PM's personal orders. No state is to feel left out.'

'Oh! In that case, I can rework the programme to include items from each state.' He was proving a tough nut to budge.

'Hmm. That would be a long programme.'

'We could keep it brief.'

'Say ten minutes per state. That is four-and-a-half hours. Sorry, Mohanty. The programme for Shah is a packed one. Can't spare the time. Good idea, though.'

'Wait, wait. We could break up the programme and try to fit it in when he has some spare time.'

'Mohanty, the schedule is really tight. I can squeeze in a minute or two here and there, but nothing to accommodate a programme like the one you are suggesting.'

'A little bit here, a little bit there. The artistes will be very happy. They have not had anything to do for a while now. The last do was the birthday party of the speaker of the Mizoram assembly. And that was last year. He didn't invite us back this year.'

Mohanty looked as though he would start crying any moment now. I felt sorry for him. 'Look, I cannot help you this time. But the next time there is some visiting dignitary, I'll make sure you are included.'

He nodded and made as if to leave. I sent up a silent prayer of thanks. Prematurely, it turned out. He turned back. 'Look, I have an idea.'

Oh, shit.

'Shah is here to watch the cricket match, no?'

'Yes.'

'Then we can organize something before play starts and during the breaks. Five days' play. There should be plenty of time. We can do it on the field. No need for a stage or special facilities.'

'What?'

'Yes, yes. Don't you think it is a wonderful idea?'

I was floored and couldn't think of anything to say. Sort of like being winded by a right from Mike Tyson. 'Wait, wait. There is the security aspect.'

'Don't worry. I'll liaise with the SPG chaps.'

'They might want to eat or chat during the breaks.'

8

The American President Calls

1

'Sir...'

'What? What? What?'

It was two in the morning. The Old Man was fast asleep. I had been fast asleep as well until I was woken up by some external affairs type. Night desk, I suppose. There had been an urgent call from the US embassy. The President of the United States had decided to call the Old Man. Time for the call: 2am. Why the President couldn't consult the CIA or some such to figure out what the time was in India was beyond me. Probably too busy upholding truth, justice and the American way of life (I refuse to dignify their motto by using capitals).

In any event, I couldn't take liberties with the President of the United States. Trying the sort of stunt I pulled on Shah would probably mean a Tomahawk cruise missile or some close cousin thereof through my roof. All, needless to say, in the name of truth, justice and all that rot.

So here I was, attempting to rouse the Old Man.

'Sir, please, sir.'

'What? What's the time?'

'Two in the morning, sir.'

'What? Oh my God, he is attacking us!'

'Sir....'

'Swami, why did you go and pull his leg like this? Now he is coming and attacking us! You should have known that Punjabis don't like to be insulted by Madrasis like you.'

'I am not a Madrasi, sir. I am a Tamilian.'

'Tamil, Madras, all the same. You are all idiots. Now you have started a war. My God! Which city is he attacking? Is he attacking Delhi?'

'Sir....'

'My God! Has the army been alerted? Do the generals know about this? My God! My clothes, my clothes. I cannot address the nation dressed in my pyjamas.'

'Listen to me, sir....'

'Have they bombed the Doordarshan studios? My God! Then I shall have to broadcast on radio. Quick, call the car! I can talk on the radio in my pyjamas. Damn you, Madrasis!'

'There is no war, sir,' I shouted. The Old Man was close to hysterics.

'What? What?'

'There is no war, sir.'

'Then why did you wake me up? Damn Madrasi!'

'Sir, I resent these repeated insults to Tamil Nadu and Tamilians. I shall resign and inform the country of the reason for the resignation.'

'Arre, arre, don't be silly. See, Hema Malini is a Madrasi and I like her. Just joking, you see. But why did you wake me up?'

'Sir, the President of America is to call any minute.'

'Hain?'

'The President of America, sir.. He has sent word through his embassy that he will be calling.'

As if on cue, the phone rang. 'Stand by please, the President of the United States will be with you shortly.' A confident American voice, one used to dragging all and sundry out of bed at two in the morning.

I stood by, as did the Old Man. He looked too stunned to speak.

'This is the President of the United States.'

I cannot deny that a frisson of excitement ran through me. It is not every day that I get to chat with the President of the United States.

'Good morning, sir. The Prime Minister is standing by. Here he is.' I handed over the phone and withdrew to another room where I could listen in on an extension.

'Hey, Mr Prime Minister, how are ya?'

'I am begging your pardon?'

'How you doin'?'

'I am eighty-two years old, you see, and suffering from a variety of ailments. The doctors have prescribed a good night's sleep.'

'Nothin' like a good night's sleep with the wife, eh?'

'My wife has passed away, sir.'

'I'm sorry to hear that, sir, I really am.'

'Your CIA didn't inform you?'

'Nah. They keep busy with important things, the CIA.'

'If I may ask, what are these important things?'

'Truth, justice and the American way of life, in a nutshell.'

'Oh. They have not informed you of terrorism in Kashmir?'

'Can't say that they have.'

'Then let me update you. Pakistan is not living up to its commitments as agreed to in the Shimla Agreement. They are fermenting terrorism in Kashmir, which, as you know, is Indian territory.'

'That's terrible. It really is.'

'Yes, yes. It is creating grave difficulties. But we are committed to upholding human rights.'

'Attaboy! That's the kinda thing I like to hear. Now listen, Mr Prime Minister, my wife and I would like to visit the Taj Mahal some time.'

'It would be my pleasure to welcome you as a guest. Would you like to see a cricket match too?'

'Can't say that I do.'

'It is a very interesting game. In fact, the Prime Minister of Pakistan is coming here shortly to witness a test match, that is, a game of cricket. He is to be my guest.'

'That's very nice. But I'll stick to the Taj Mahal if you don't mind. But hey, didn't ya tell me that the Pakistanis are terrorists?'

'Yes, sir, but we believe in non-violence. As Jesus Christ said, we turn the other cheek.'

'Great, great. Jesus Christ is my hero, my main man. Now listen, you tell that Pakistani to lay off, will ya? I don't like terrorists myself. Now take care and I'm looking forward to seeing the Taj Mahal.'

'I look forward to having you as my guest, sir.'

2

For someone who had been semi-hysterical just a few moments earlier, the Old Man had acquitted himself wonderfully. Our so-called foreign policy mandarins, those overrated jokers from the IFS, could not have turned matters to our advantage as deftly and with as little fuss as the Old Man had at two in the morning. I could barely refrain from hugging him.

For someone who had just made a great breakthrough in our relations with the World's Greatest Superpower, he remained remarkably composed and sober. Me, I'd have been jumping up and down, yelling attaboy from the rooftops. Instead, all he said was this:

'Swami, I want to go back to sleep. You follow up about this Taj Mahal business. And what I said about Madrasis, I didn't mean it. So, you forget about it. No more resignation tamashas from you.'

I couldn't wait for dawn to break. Shah could stay in Paharganj for all I cared. The President of the United States was coming, arrangements needed to be made, things needed to be taken care of. Pronto. There was also this matter of breaking the news to the world press.

There had been a tectonic shift in international relations and the world had to be told about it.

3

'What? I don't believe it!'

My chum, Neeta, over at External Affairs (and not a bad sort despite being from the IFS) was a long-time cold war warrior. One who sang paeans to the Non-Aligned Movement in this, the twenty-first century.

'You'd better believe it. I heard it from the President's mouth. Read his lips, metaphorically speaking.'

'Don't you think we need to double-check things?'

'Neeta, you are not talking about some low-level state department flunkey. You are talking about the President of the United States.'

'That's just the point. He is known for shooting off his mouth and doesn't really mean what he says. I think we should double-check.'

'Check, double-check. The President of the United States wants to visit the Taj Mahal and you want to double-check. He has denounced Pakistan in no uncertain terms, he has supported us on Kashmir, and all you want to do is double-check. Look, Neeta, you can double-check in your spare time. What we need now is action. I want a meeting here in – let's see – two hours' time. Your secretary, the head of the US desk, we can patch in our ambassador in Washington. I'll contact Home, Defence, Commerce, Tourism, Information and Broadcasting – all to be here in two hours' time. Agenda, dates, itinerary, the works. We will shock the Yanks with our efficiency. See you here.'

I hung up.

4

Getting Official New Delhi to move pronto is tough, but I was up to it. There was much grumbling about missed tea breaks and important meetings. Important meetings, my arse. There was nothing quite as important as the President of the United States and I wielded the whip mercilessly.

Fixit Dixit could have learnt a few lessons in fixing things.

A trickle at first, in greater numbers later, the conference room filled up as the appointed hour approached. They came in carrying files, briefcases, laptops – the essentials of a modern and responsive bureaucracy. The public might make noises from time to time about the steel frame outliving its utility, but they are ignorant of the inner workings of government and it isn't for nothing that they are known as the great unwashed masses. There was a sense of anticipation in the air, a sense of quiet purpose and determination.

I looked up – they were all here bar External Affairs. Where the hell were they? I decided to give them a couple of minutes and, when they still hadn't made an appearance, called the meeting to order.

It is always useful to establish authority at the outset and this I did in my introductory remarks.

'Ladies and gentlemen, there have been significant developments overnight regarding our relations with the United States. Suffice it to say that there has been a quantum leap in the state of our relations. A personal element has added an element of trust and added insights into our perceptions of geopolitical realities. Over the next few days, you will be getting details of realignments in geopolitical blocks as well as fresh insights into international relations. This is all very important, but a mere preamble to the purpose of this meeting – to coordinate all aspects of a visit to India by the President of the United States.'

There was a buzz around the room as the import of my words sunk in. The door to the room opened and Neeta slunk in. Alone.

I glared at her, but she didn't seem in the least put out. She gestured, indicating that I should step out. Something about her, the look on her face perhaps, told me that it was best not to stand on formality.

'Please excuse me a moment, ladies and gentlemen,' I said before following Neeta out. Some others had noticed her at the door, and as I stepped out, I could hear the low murmur of puzzled gossip.

'Swami, it is not on.'

'What is not on?'

'The Prez visiting the Taj Mahal. It is not on.'

I stared at her. She was being unusually obtuse.

'Neeta,' I spoke slowly, as to a retarded child. 'As I told you this morning, I was privy to the conversation. It is not a question of the Old Man misunderstanding. I heard the President with my very ears.'

'Swami, what you told me goes against everything that the US has been telling us for years.'

'Neeta, the cold war is over. We are in a new era. There is a new paradigm in international relations.'

'Swami, will you just listen and stop this paradigm nonsense? After you spoke to me, I called up the US ambassador. He knew nothing about a phone call last night. He checked with his people. There was no phone call from them to EA last night.'

'But...'

'Stop butting in and let me finish. That is point one. Point two. There was no one in EA last night.'

'But your night desk...?'

'Swami, we don't have a night desk.'

'Then...?'

'It looks, Swami, as though someone has pulled a prank on you.'

'But the person I spoke to...'

'The ambassador was good enough to check back with Washington. The State Department confirms that there was no call from the White House, that there has been no suggestion to the White House about a visit, that there is no plan for a visit to India, period. You had better go in and tell them that the visit has been cancelled.'

I stared at her dumbfounded. 'What am I supposed to tell the Old Man? He hates being woken up and when he hears that someone has pulled a fast one... God! I think I'm done for! What a mess! Oh my God!'

She looked at me with something akin to pity. 'Swami, I could give you a lecture on geopolitical realities, but I'll refrain. I suggest you call off the meeting and tell the Old Man that the President has a cold or something and has put things off indefinitely.'

Damn! Now I owed her one.

5

I have to say that I don't like having my leg pulled. This particular instance, however, was not merely a personal humiliation, but a potential threat to geopolitical realities. Our relationship with the world's superpower had always been a prickly one, thanks to Neeta and her non-aligned colleagues, and a piece of idiocy like this could very easily tip things down the path of no return. I was torn between the desire to root out the pranksters and make an example of them and the more politic course of swallowing my pride and letting things lie.

There were some practical questions as well. A formal inquiry would mean the Old Man's acquiescence and the inevitable disclosure that I had woken him up for no good reason. That the pranksters had almost pulled it off would become public knowledge. The newspaper cartoonists would have a field day and I could look forward to many letters and telephone calls from people claiming to be the President of the United States. Not a very pleasing prospect.

Ignoring the whole thing was not an option either. They knew that they had pulled one over me. They knew that they had suckered the Old Man into his usual inanities about terrorism and Kashmir. They could not be expected to lie low and refrain from another breach of our defences. Above all, they would have had, and probably were still having, a good laugh behind our backs. Again, not something I could contemplate with equanimity.

I also knew that news of the quickly aborted meeting would get around and questions would be raised about why the meeting had needed to be convened in such a hurry – questions that would quickly lead to discussions about Swami's competence.

I was an envied man, I knew, and envy does not make for healthy working relations. Envy coupled with a perception of weakness was a lethal combination and this was what I was up against. I had to do something.

It was a problem that would have given Chanakya pause for thought.

It gave me pause for thought.

6

I picked up the phone with a sense of trepidation. I was putting myself in another's hands and the outcome was not one I could predict.

Jugal Kishore Hansraj, as his name might expect you to believe, was a dope who had been at the same school as me. He had tilted mightily against the IAS windmill to little avail: His third and final attempt had netted him a post in the Department of Telecommunications. There, he had made do with the odd promotion. More recently, he had been after me. Surely, as his old schoolmate, I could do something for him. I had given him the brush-off time and again, but circumstances now forced me into a re-evaluation of realities.

'You want what?'

I had outlined my requirements: I needed calls to my house and to 7 Race Course Drive to be traced to their source. Now I had to repeat myself to this dumb DoT timeserver. Once again, I had this sense of doing the wrong thing, but it was too late to back out.

'Not possible, yaar.'

'What do you mean, not possible? Don't you have computerized exchanges, computerized billing? It should be easy for you to trace calls.'

'It is very difficult. Getting into computers and all. Great technical difficulties.'

'I know you can do it, Jugal Kishore.'

'Arre yaar, bahut kaam hai. Yeh sab mein bahut time lagega. Technical difficulties.'

'Then tell me how you trace calls from Dawood Ibrahim to his chums in Mumbai.'

'That is CBI work.'

'You mean they know how to get stuff from your computers, but you don't?'

'I am not saying that. What I am saying is that is *their* work. I have administrative responsibilities.'

'Arre, Jugal Kishore, I called you at eleven, you were at your tea break. At twelve-thirty, you were at your lunch break. At two, you were still at your lunch break. At three, you had left for your tea break. Now I've finally got you at four-thirty.'

'Field visit. We are not like you IAS types. Sit behind your desks like sahibs, cannot help old friends from school. We have field visit work. Telecommunicating India is our motto.'

Ah! Now we were on a common wavelength. 'Jugal Kishore, you know sometimes it is not possible. Sometimes it is. But I am always willing to bend over backwards for an old friend.'

There was a snort over the line that I ignored.

'Now again, what was that you wanted?'

For the third time, I explained. There was a pause before he replied, 'Under the Telecommunications Act, a magistrate's order has to be...'

'I know all that. This cannot go to a magistrate. National security.'

He went on as if I hadn't interrupted. 'In cases where matters pertaining to national security are concerned, an order from a justice of the Supreme Court has to be obtained vide section...'

'Jugal Kishore, if I wanted to go to the Supreme Court, I wouldn't be calling you.'

'Then you are asking me to commit an illegality.'

'You, too, were asking for an out-of-turn transfer. Under the Government of India Rules of Service section...'

'Yes, yes. I know all that.'

'Then you were asking me to commit an illegality.'

'I know that. But you just said that you were willing to bend over backwards for an old friend.'

'Yes, yes, yes. So what do you want?'

'There is this opening in the ITU ... '

'ITU?'

'International Telecommunications Union – in Geneva.'

The bastard wanted a posting in Geneva! I was stunned at his effrontery. 'Look, Jugal Kishore...'

'My daughter, she is entering an impressionable age. Delhi is a terrible place – too many Punjabi boys. I want her to go to a good finishing school in Geneva.'

What was the world coming to? 'Now look here, I am sure that only senior personnel can be considered...'

'Swami, what you are asking me to do is prima facie illegal. What I am asking you to do is unusual, but not prima facie illegal – only bending over backwards for an old friend.'

'But...'

'Besides, if the press got to know about it...'

'You've got a deal: I get my info, you get the posting.'

'No, my friend. I get the posting, you get the info.'

He had me over a barrel. There was nothing to do but capitulate. My just rewards for dealing with the Jugal Kishore Hansrajs of the world. Now all I could do was hope he would live up to his end of the bargain and not talk to the press.

I had this ominous feeling that I was losing my touch.

7

I had recurring nightmares the next few days, all featuring Jugal Kishore Hansraj: JKH urinating against the sides of the Palais des Nations; JKH depositing his chewed pan along the shores of Lake Geneva; JKH travelling ticketless in the trams in Geneva; JKH opening his mouth at ITU meetings...

JKH, late of Bulandshahr, now a representative of India in Europe's most cosmopolitan city.

I sweated through the nights and fought off distracting thoughts during the days, knowing that it would take just one faux pas for fingers to be pointed at me. Though a myriad decisions awaited my attention each morning, my distracted mind could only wait for the other shoe to drop. The days dragged on, the pranksters remained elusive, and I had visions of JKH's daughter attempting to learn how to use a knife and fork at her finishing school.

She was probably not the only Indian there. Switzerland was a happy hunting ground for bureaucrats on their foreign postings. There were a good number of UN organizations there and the salaries were tax-free and the banks were good. There were also any number of good finishing schools. Most of those there were IAS chaps. They knew their Ps and Qs and their knives and forks, they spoke good English, they knew how to dress. Now think of the JKH family, the undiluted essence of Bulandshahr.

I thought of them. Often. He had his posting. My info remained elusive.

9

Sandalwood Capers

1

Fate has a tendency to strike when a man is down. Shah's visit was only days away and Delhi was preening itself in anticipation. There was a buzz in the air, a heightened sense of anticipation that I was aware of, but did not feel. All courtesy JKH, who hadn't bothered to call even once.

'Mr Swami?' Long distance from the sound of it. Not JKH, though. Wrong accent.

'Yes.'

'Mr Swami of the Prime Minister's Office?'

'Yes, yes,' I said impatiently.

'Sir, I am calling from Dharmapuri. In Tamil Nadu.'

'I know that Dharmapuri is in Tamil Nadu. Who are you and what do you want?'

'Sir, there appears to be a problem, sir.'

'Yes, yes. What is it?'

'Sir, myself, I am Pughazendan, inspector of police.'

'Yes.'

'Posted in Dharmapuri.'

'You've already told me that.'

'Now it appears that there is a problem.'

'Listen, Inspector Pughazendan. Stop wasting my time. What is the problem?'

'Sorry, sir, for the wasting of your time. But the problem is as follows. You are aware, sir, that the Satyamangalam forests are nearby, lying to the west. One Veerappan, sandalwood smuggler, elephant poacher and murderer, operates with a gang of brigands in these forests.'

'Yes, I know that.'

'Routine patrols are organized to prevent the smuggling of sandalwood. One such patrol headed by Constable Moovendan was on patrol yesterday. Upon receiving information, a trap was laid and certain miscreants apprehended red-handed.'

'You mean you caught Veerappan? You must be congratulated.'

'No sir, no sir. There appears to be some misapprehension on your part. It was not Veerappan who was apprehended. It was one Ravanan, a charge-sheeter previously detained under the Goondas Act. He had in his possession at the time of apprehension two hundred and forty kilos of sandalwood.'

'He was carrying all that?' I was incredulous.

'No, sir. It was loaded onto a commercial vehicle, an Ashok Leyland Cargo 709 model, bearing the registration number TN 37 A 0359. We have ascertained that this is a false registration number. The vehicle has been detained under the provisions of the Motor Vehicles Act.'

'Inspector Pugazhendan, I appreciate your bringing me up to date on this matter, but this is the PMO and we have no administrative interest in matters of this nature. I suggest you call your state government in Chennai for further guidance.'

'Yes, sir, but it appears that there is a problem.'

'What problem?'

'You see, sir, the apprehended miscreant, Ravanan by name, is claiming that the sandalwood was for a special order coming from the PMO itself.'

'What?'

'Yes, sir. Now you see the reason for my apprehension.'

'Let me assure you, Inspector, that there has been no such order from the PMO and that I know of no Ravanan. You may proceed with his apprehension as per your standard procedures.'

This was bizarre and even took my mind off JKH for a few minutes. It was clear that this Ravanan was a resourceful fellow, dragging the PMO into his sordid activities. But he hadn't reckoned with the good Inspector Pughazendan. He must have assumed that the mere mention of the PMO would have reduced the inspector to an abject, apologetic, apology of an inspector.

Good for Inspector Pughazendan, I thought, and there I thought the matter rested.

2

'Swami?'

It was Suresh, a chum over at NDTV.

'Yes?'

'You had better watch our news.'

It was a story they had picked up from one of the Tamil channels. A huge pile of sandalwood off to one side, someone with a fierce looking moustache being led off by the cops, yelling at the cameras. Ravanan. His story, shorn of the histrionics, was this: He had been asked by the PMO to construct a huge sandalwood sofa. They had baulked at the cost and had asked him to find a cheaper supplier of sandalwood. He had. Now he was being arrested for following the PMO's orders. He was upset at the injustice done to him.

It was a good story, well told. (If you had seen Ravanan in action, you too would have agreed that the story was told well. In fact, you would have agreed that he was misplaced as a sandalwood smuggler. Tamil filmdom might well have found a replacement for Sivaji Ganesan. But that is a matter which does not concern this story.)

It was a shit-hitting-fan sort of story. All the ingredients were there: hints of malfeasance and misplaced priorities in high places, an angle which included abuse of the environment and deliberate connivance in the same by highly-placed officials, and best of all, a story that had a germ of truth at its heart.

The sofa.

I did what I could. An official denial that a sandalwood sofa had been ordered. An official denial that anything had been said about cheaper sources of sandalwood. (A matter of logic, this: If there was no sandalwood sofa to begin with, where was the question of sourcing cheap sandalwood?) An official denial that the PMO had anything to do with Ravanan. Dark hints that this was all part of an opposition conspiracy.

I thought I had made some headway when I was blindsided by an interview with the BCCI chief. The very same sleazebag, you will remember, who cost the Old Man the Chhattisgarh election. There he was, a bland look concealing the most labyrinthine of minds, talking with a reporter.

'Yes,' he said. 'I can confirm that a super sofa, designed to seat forty or fifty, was ordered by the PMO. They wanted all the ministers to watch this match. You can well imagine all the practical problems this has caused. Good paying customers have been turned away to accommodate these ministers who, as you can well imagine, are not paying one paisa for the privilege of watching this important match. Now, each minister is insisting on bringing his or her Z category security along. You can well imagine the chaos this will cause. You can also well imagine how they will be standing in the way of good paying customers. And there are insurmountable technical problems as well. With this super sofa in place, where do we put the sight screen? We have appointed a technical committee headed by Sunil Gavaskar and Imran Khan to look into this problem and suggest alternatives, but they have not been able to meet because Mr Khan is yet to receive his visa. You can well imagine the problems this is causing in staging the match.'

There was more in response to some leading questions from the reporter.

Damn! To correct the story by saying that the sofa was to seat only twenty-five would be playing into his hands. Ditto denying that we had specified sandalwood for the sofa. Pointing out that Imran Khan wanted to visit Kashmir and was unwilling to accept a visa limiting him to Delhi would mean raking up an unnecessary issue. Cricket, not Kashmir, was the issue.

Having the reporter shot was a tempting alternative, but this was not Pakistan and we wouldn't get away with it.

Not for the first time I felt that what the country really needed was a period of benevolent dictatorship, possibly headed by the Old Man and assisted by me. No pesky reporters, the BCCI firmly under control, the country marching purposefully into a brighter dawn. I basked in the vision for some long moments before shaking myself back into the here and now.

The sofa story, or the Super Sofa story as the press insisted on referring to it, gathered momentum.

Shah, quiet since the buzkashi fiasco, found his voice courtesy the BBC. The bastard smirked his way through the interview. 'I am a simple man with a simple wish – to watch a game of cricket. All I need is a simple chair, no super sofas. Certainly no sandalwood super sofas. I am aware that the sandalwood tree is an endangered species and would do nothing to further endanger it. I appeal to the Indian government not to cut down sandalwood trees for my sake. A simple chair is all I ask for. And, of course, a visa for Imran Khan.'

The Super Sofa made it to CNN, MSNBC and Fox News.

Closer home, there was much about Ravanan and his sandalwood source, Veerappan. Chikkaveeraraja decided that the waters needed muddying and offered to provide sandalwood from the Karnataka government stocks – to protect the nation's precious heritage, of course.

And yes, there were the obligatory self-immolations in Tamil Nadu, protesting the discriminatory treatment meted out to their sandalwood.

Another day, Indian style.

The Old Man, after giving me dirty looks all day, had himself admitted into hospital. And once more it was me, Swami, holding off the barbarian hordes.

3

I must admit that it was not a prospect that I could face with equanimity. Half-truths are the worst nightmare for someone in my position – one finds oneself on a slippery slope with little to hang on to. These are also the times when one's buddies conveniently disappear. Life, in times like these, is not worth living.

I thought quite seriously about quitting – an ashram in Rishikesh, where one spends one's days chanting in the shadows of the Himalayas had its attractions. I even put in a call to the Paramacharya, but he was off meditating somewhere in the High Himalayas.

This I took as a sign. Perhaps it was not yet time to quit. Perhaps I was meant to fight this battle as well, much as I had held off the hordes in the past. I paused to take stock.

Negatives: time. Things could always be managed, given time. People were human, they had their foibles, they could be dealt with. Given time. Then there was the Old Man. The trip to the hospital was a clear signal of his displeasure and his lack of willingness to lend his political weight to the cause. If I was unable to pull the irons out of the fire, he would let the fire consume me. Then the obvious solution: cancelling the sofa quietly and making do with some plastic chairs. But that was out of the question. The Old Man would never consent to having his backside rest in a plastic chair. Those bloody ministers wanted to share a sofa with Shah, not merely occupy plastic chairs in his vicinity. And finally, changing now meant acceding to Shah's suggestion. Acceding to a public Pakistani suggestion was a no-no – it revealed weakness and a lack of resolve. To summarize, the difficulties were formidable.

Positives: um... well... let's just say that I felt as Napoleon must have when he woke up on the morning of Waterloo with an attack of piles. Napoleon at least could have popped down to Paharganj to consult a piles and fistula specialist.

I had only my wits about me.

4

After much thought, I decided on a multipronged approach.

The BCCI chief, first. I had the home ministry ask for a list of all the ticket-holders in the stadium pavilion, citing security concerns. Pronto, of course. I had the finance ministry ask for all the accounts pertaining to the ticket sales. I had the I&B ministry ask for all the details of the broadcasting and uplifting contracts entered into by the BCCI. I had the Cable Operators Association of Delhi threaten to boycott the match citing the extortionate fees charged by the broadcasters.

All this before lunch.

I treated myself to a leisurely lunch at the Meridien. Scampi with sundried tomatoes in a white wine sauce, fresh Norwegian salmon in a dill butter sauce, a cappuccino. I had thought of asking Neeta to join me, but decided against it. External Affairs was always complaining about their budgetary allocation and, in any event, I did not feel like discussing Imran Khan's visa problem over lunch.

As anticipated, the BCCI chief called in my absence. Thrice, no less. Time to turn up the heat on the bastard. I had Finance organize an income tax raid on his house and premises and Environment begin an investigation on his mining activities in Chhattisgarh.

In the meanwhile, I asked for all the files on the sofa. Someone had been playing games and I needed to know just what was going on.

Early afternoon, and the telephone calls from the BCCI chief were now coming in every five minutes. I let him dangle. Instead, I called Inspector Pughazendan. I needed to know how the Tamil TV channel had got to Ravanan that quickly. There was something fishy in the way the story had been picked up, something that meant one thing and one thing only – dirty politics.

Pughazendan was not very forthcoming at first. No surprise, really. The sod was probably already in trouble for calling me up and did not want to compound the felony by passing on more information. The Old Man and the Tamil Nadu CM had never been the best of chums and neither would let go of a chance to show up the other. I sensed the CM's hand in this, but needed more than a mere whiff of suspicion.

Pughazendan stonewalled manfully. He had merely done his job arresting the alleged miscreant, Ravanan, who had been in the process of absconding with the loot when caught red-handed. The arrest had been made based on information received; he couldn't divulge his source without consulting his superiors. He didn't know who had tipped off the TV crew. They had shown up just when Ravanan was being remanded into custody. I was sorely tempted to throw the book at him, but I didn't need a Centre–State fracas at this juncture. The alternative, given that I hadn't all year to get things straightened out, was a rather heavy handed resort to threats.

Threats are not my currency: I find them distasteful, ungentlemanly, crude, the very antithesis of what I, an IAS officer, stand for. But the situation makes the man and I was forced to use what tools were readily at hand – with a heavy heart, of course.

I let Pughazendan know that my next telephone call would be to the Tamil Nadu CM, thanking him for the exemplary cooperation extended to the PMO by Inspector Pughazendan. This got his undivided attention as I knew it would and the sordid facts were soon laid bare.

The TV crew had showed up with a letter from a minister. They had all headed for a remote part of the district, where the alleged miscreant had been waiting. Three retakes had to be gone through at the police station before the TV crew pronounced themselves satisfied. Ravanan, well fed on chicken curry while in custody, was due to escape the next day while being taken to court.

A little more persuasion and the details of the proposed escape became clear. The guards were to stop for a leak and Ravanan was to make good his escape. The guards would be suspended with much fanfare and reinstated with little fuss later in the day.

I was stunned. Stunned at this cavalier disregard of the law. Stunned at this casual flouting of democratic norms. Stunned at this exercise in political cynicism. I had seen a lot in my years in government, but this left me shaken and appalled. Action was called for, swift, direct action, and Centre–State relations be damned. I set the machinery in motion.

5

It was the day after my conversation with Inspector Pughazendan. The BCCI chief had flown into Delhi and had – cheeky bastard! – attempted to enter the Old Man's hospital room. Timely intervention on my part foiled his plan and he was now in my anteroom cooling his heels. He could wait: Operation Ravanan was under way.

I must admit that I was nervous. There were a thousand things that could have gone wrong, a thousand tiny details that could have tripped up the whole thing. I swallowed innumerable cups of coffee and puffed away on cigarettes until the phone rang with the news that Ravanan was in the bag. I had arranged a counter-ambush with a bunch of BSF jawans and ensured that Ravanan's freedom was a fleeting one. He was soon on a plane to Delhi, a debriefing session under way even as the Air Force AN 22 rolled down the runway en route to Delhi.

Ravanan, it turned out, was a minor party functionary and had been promised a Rajya Sabha seat for his part in the escapade.

My conversation with the Tamil Nadu CM was hugely satisfying. Falsifying evidence, aiding and abetting a felony, desecration of the environment: if ever there was a case for using Article 356, this was it. By the end of our conversation, I had collected so many political IOUs that I was tempted to enter politics myself. The Old Man was getting on in years and a younger hand was needed on the tiller. It was with some effort that I held back. My time would come; for now, it was as well to make the Old Man's task easier. And it had been made easier by something the Tamil Nadu CM had let slip.

6

Like the true professional sleazebag that he was, the BCCI chief was all charm, oozing unctuousness as he made his way to my desk.

'Mr Swami, how nice of you to make time for me. You must be a busy man indeed with all the preparations for the prime ministerial visit.' No mention, as you might have noted, of all those telephone calls of the previous day.

I nodded.

'And how is Mr Motwani doing? The nation holds its collective breath even as he battles for good health in the hospital.'

'You went to the hospital to see him.'

'Yes. How could I not? The very success of the first test match depends on his return to the pink of health.'

'You didn't check with me first.'

'My apologies, my profoundest apologies. I was so overcome with concern about Mr Motwani's health that I violated protocol. You know that this is not something I would do deliberately.'

'Really?'

'Oh, Mr Swami, surely you don't think that I...'

'What brings you to Delhi, Mr Pendse?'

He smiled an ingratiating smile. 'There are a few small matters.'

'Small matters? Surely you didn't need to make a trip to Delhi for some small matters.'

'Well, minor matters.'

'Minor matters?' I made a show of looking at my watch.

'There have been developments.'

'Developments?'

'Inquiries.'

'Inquiries? Surely you have nothing to hide, Mr Pendse. I'm sure you will be able to satisfactorily answer any questions that may arise.'

'Yes, yes. But, you see, it seems that these are not routine inquiries.'

I raised my eyebrows. Watching Ravanan had taught me a trick or two. 'Not routine? Hmm... I wonder if the authorities were acting on information?'

'But that is not possible. My life is an open book.'

'Really?'

'Mr Swami, you are pulling my leg.'

'I am a serious man, Mr Pendse. I don't believe in pulling people's legs.'

'Yes, yes. I apologize for the insinuation.'

'Apology accepted. Now what is it that you want from me?'

'These inquiries. You see, suddenly there have been a lot of inquiries. They are taking up so much of my time. No time to prepare for this most important test match.'

'Yes. And we are adding to your problem with a fifty- seat, super sandalwood sofa, right?'

'No, no. I have been misquoted.'

'You have?'

Mistake. Big mistake. He had gone on TV and I had taped his diatribe. I pulled out the DVD player and bunged in the CD. There he was, unctuous and self-righteous as ever, caught in eight bit colour and sixteen bit sound. He squirmed and looked like a weasel.

'Well, Mr Pendse?'

He licked his lips. 'That is not what I really meant to say.'

'What did you mean to say then?'

'That I was getting full cooperation from the government.'

'Oh.'

'That is really what I meant. You see, it had been a very busy time. Lots of work and so forth. Mind in a mess and so forth. So I mis-stated what I had to say. Really. I will call a press conference and commend the government for lending all assistance to the BCCI.'

'Ah! So it was all because you were very busy then?'

'Indeed, yes. Yes, indeed.'

'I can see that. Very busy indeed.'

'Yes, I am glad that you see my point.'

'Yes, very busy with Mr Ravanan, I take it.'

He froze, looking like a cornered rat. All the unctuousness had oozed away in a hurry. He had the look of a man staring at the business end of a ruinous proposition. Which, in a sense, he was.

'I'm not sure I understand.' His voice had dropped to a hoarse whisper; he smelt of defeat.

'Mr Pendse, Ravanan in on a plane winging its way to Delhi even as we speak. Having considered his position and his options, he has chosen to speak. I'm sure the news channels will have plenty to air tonight.'

What the Tamil Nadu CM had let slip was that Pendse was the brains behind the Ravanan caper. Which, in turn, was to pave the way for a split of the GNC. Why these extreme measures? The information and broadcasting minister had insisted on Doordarshan carrying the telecast of the test series. Cricket, it seemed, was more important than the march of the country towards a brighter tomorrow.

Cornered and humbled, Pendse had nothing left with which to bargain.

I was able to report to the Old Man as follows:

1. The defection of thirty-six MLAs in the Chhattisgarh assembly, reducing the incumbent government to a minority.
2. The addition of the Tamil Nadu CM's party, the ABCDEFGDMK, to the GNC, further bolstering its majority.
3. A full apology by the BCCI chief, carried by all TV channels, ending in his resignation.
4. A full retraction of the sandalwood super sofa story by the BCCI chief.
5. A clear statement by the BCCI chief denouncing Imran Khan's bid to politicize the Kashmir issue.
6. The cancellation of the Sunil Gavaskar–Imran Khan technical committee in view of the satisfactory resolution of the sofa issue.
7. The transferring of the Chhattisgarh mining concession to a party acceptable to the GNC.
8. The cancellation of allotment of all pavilion tickets and reallotment of the same to MPs belonging to the GNC and their families.
9. The donation of a Mercedes Benz car by the BCCI for the use of the Prime Minister of India.

In view of all this, the Old Man pleased all his admirers and followers by recovering fully from his illness and resuming the reins of power. You might have seen me on TV as I helped him into his new Mercedes Benz and accompanied him home.

'Swami,' he said as we drove through New Delhi. 'You have done well.'

I thought for a moment of taking advantage of the situation and pressing for a Padma Bhushan, but decided against it. There would be other opportunities to prove my worth and, who knows, perhaps do even better than a mere Padma Bhushan.

10

The Goat

1

We – the Old Man and I – were watching television. Shah had called up earlier to tell us that he would be holding a press conference and that he had a very pleasant surprise in store for us. I was suspicious. Shah had this very nasty habit of throwing curve balls at his press conferences. As a matter of abundant precaution, I had our publicity chaps on full alert. The Old Man was more sanguine. He had seen it all and little could shake him from his sense of well-being. Besides, he had a bolthole in the form of the hospital and a personal secretary who had grown adept at facing the music.

The stage was Islamic green. A green backdrop, a green carpet, a table covered with a green table-cloth, green upholstered chairs – it all looked– like a scene from *The Wizard of Oz*.

A cluster of microphones sat on the table awaiting the great man and a bunch of journalists sat around the room doing the same.

There was a bustle and Shah strode onto the stage. He cleared his throat, looked around acknowledging a favoured journalist or two before reading from a prepared text.

'Gentlemen and ladies, my fellow Pakistanis. We are now only days away from an event of considerable historical significance. Relations between India and Pakistan have been adversarial for too long and I hope to bring about a qualitative change with my visit to New Delhi. I am happy that the Government of India has gone out of its way to arrange an interesting programme. I take this as a sign that the Indians too want a change in the way we have dealt with each other. Inshallah, our citizens can look forward to years of prosperity, rather than war or acrimony.

'Now, on behalf of all Pakistanis, I would like to make a very special gesture to all Indians. When I go to India, I will be taking with me –'

here he paused and gestured. The cameras duly swivelled around and focused on a goat.

Shah continued:

'– this mountain goat from the Baltistan area of Pakistan to present to Prime Minister Motwani. We have named him Sikander. This is a rare and prized specimen and its rarity symbolizes our desire for peace and friendship with India.'

The rare and prized specimen had that vacant look so characteristic of goats. Sikander clearly did not relish the limelight. Twice he tried to break away, once coming close to goring Shah's arse before being wrestled away. Overcome by the trauma, he crapped all over the green carpet.

I turned to see what the Old Man's reaction was to all this. He had gone to sleep. I turned back to look at the goat. I am no zoologist and, to my eye, it looked like any old goat. Well, it had a rather distinguished looking beard and the hooves had tufts of hair sticking out behind, but these were mere details. The fact of the matter was this: Sikander was a goat and, in the name of friendship and so forth, the Pakistanis were dumping him on us.

I wasn't sure whether to laugh or feel insulted. I wasn't even sure how I should brief the publicity honchos. Was Shah pulling a fast one on us? Would we look like asses if we publicly welcomed the gesture? Would it be churlish to turn the goat down? Were we supposed to eat it or preserve it at the Delhi Zoo?

On screen, Sikander broke away once more and tried to hump the table. His handlers decided that they had had enough and wrestled him off stage. The show over, Shah followed Sikander offstage.

The Old Man let go a gentle snore. Now, on top of everything else, I had the problem of the goat to deal with.

2

Minutes of the Ad Hoc Committee instituted to look into the question of the goat to be presented by His Excellency, the Prime Minister of Pakistan to the Prime Minister of India:

Location: Shastri Bhawan, New Delhi
Date: 20 November

Present:
Cabinet secretary
Home secretary
Foreign secretary
Secretary, Department of Animal Husbandry
Secretary, Department of Environment and Urban Affairs
Secretary, Department of Legal Affairs
Secretary, Department of Civil Aviation
Special invitees:
Personal secretary to the Prime Minister

The following questions were raised during the aforesaid discussion:

1. In view of the regulations regarding import of animals, can the said animal be imported without relevant permission and inoculation?
2. In view of the potential for disease carried by the said animal, should the aircraft bearing the animal not be fumigated on landing on Indian territory?

3. In view of the fact that Baltistan is part of Indian territory, currently under illegal occupation by Pakistan, would accepting the said animal be tantamount to de facto recognition of the Line of Control (LOC)?

4. In view of the fact that goats are considered common animals which, as such, do not constitute an endangered species, is such a gift acceptable, in terms of protocol, to the Prime Minister of India?

5. In view of the gift sought to be presented to the PM, should a reciprocal gift be considered? In case a decision is reached to make a reciprocal gesture, a decision regarding an appropriate gift needs to be made.

6. In the event that the Government of India chooses to accept the gift of the said animal, a suitable venue for the said transaction needs to be agreed upon.

7. In view of the unruly behaviour of the said animal witnessed on numerous cable TV channels, and should the answer to Item 4 above be decided as acceptable, the need for adequate precautions to protect the PM and his entourage from any untoward eventualities needs to be taken into account when Item 6 above is considered.

8. In view of the potential importance to bilateral relations of the aforesaid transaction, the need for adequate media coverage cannot be

overemphasized. It is therefore considered appropriate to entrust coverage to Doordarshan with the proviso that other channels desirous of broadcasting the said transaction can purchase footage from Doordarshan.

9. In view of Item 8 above, the need for adequate remuneration for Doordarshan needs to be considered.

10. In view of the long history of perfidious actions by Pakistan, the need to ensure that the goat is not a Trojan horse of some kind – that is, laden with explosives or monitoring devices – is paramount.

With a view to developing answers and suggestions regarding Items 1-10 above, it was decided to constitute the following subcommittees to consider the questions as hereunder:

Items 1 and 2. Secretary of animal husbandry, secretary of environment and urban affairs, secretary of civil aviation, superintendent of Delhi Zoo (special invitee), Ms Maneka Gandhi (special invitee), personal secretary to Prime Minister (ex-officio secretary to subcommittee).

Items 3 and 4. Foreign secretary, secretary of legal affairs, cabinet secretary, Mr I.K. Gujral (special invitee), personal secretary to the Prime Minister (ex-officio secretary to subcommittee).

Item 5. Cabinet secretary, secretary of animal husbandry, secretary of environment and urban affairs, superintendent of Delhi Zoo (special invitee), Ms Maneka Gandhi (special invitee), personal secretary to Prime Minister (ex-officio secretary to subcommittee).

Item 6. Foreign secretary, cabinet secretary, chief minister of Delhi (special invitee), personal secretary to Prime Minister (ex-officio secretary to subcommittee).

Item 7. Home secretary, foreign secretary, Mr Salman Khan (special invitee), inspector general of police, Delhi (special invitee), personal secretary to Prime Minister (ex-officio secretary to subcommittee).

Item 8. Secretary of information and broadcasting, cabinet secretary, Mr Amitabh Bachchan (special invitee), Mr Prannoy Roy (special invitee), Ms Ekta Kapoor (special invitee), personal secretary to Prime Minister (ex-officio secretary to subcommittee).

Item 9. Secretary of information and broadcasting, finance secretary, cabinet secretary, personal secretary to Prime Minister (ex-officio secretary to subcommittee).

Item 10 (to be constituted in secret). Head, RAW, head, IB, head, CBI, home secretary. No ex-officio secretary in view of the sensitivities involved. Home secretary to act as ex-officio secretary. Meetings to be held in camera.

The eight (8) subcommittees constituted hereto to deliberate on matters allocated to them and report back to the Ad Hoc Committee at the earliest.

Meeting was adjourned.

3

As you can see, I had work to do. Meetings to be scheduled, agendas set, refreshments arranged for, the sort of thing that would reduce the average man on the street to despair, the sort of thing the average IAS officer does without thinking a dozen times each day.

Amitabh Bachchan and Ekta Kapoor cried off citing prior commitments, Prannoy Roy and Maneka Gandhi cried off citing conflicts of interest, Salman Khan was shooting on location in the South Pacific and could not be contacted. That left only I.K. Gujral and the superintendent of the Delhi Zoo among the special invitees.

I must say that I was a touch disappointed: I had been looking forward to rubbing shoulders with Ekta Kapoor and sharing colas with Messrs Bachchan and Khan. Not to mention exchanging thoughts on the proper diet for lactating dogs with Maneka Gandhi. Fact is, I had always been fascinated by dogs and the obedience they display towards their masters and mistresses and had often wondered how such habits could be encouraged in the lower reaches of the country's bureaucracy. It has been my contention for some time now that the diet fed to lactating bitches has a bearing on filial obedience among canines. Now this discussion would have to wait.

Scheduling a meeting involving senior bureaucrats is no easy task. There were luncheon appointments, golf tee-off times, trips to London and Washington, not to mention fires lit by politicians that needed to be doused.

Having scheduled a meeting and having got everyone around a table didn't mean that I was home free. The finance secretary, for instance, was given to holding forth on partridges. The home secretary had undertaken a detailed study of Verse 23 of the Bhagvad Gita in his spare time and considered it his bounden duty to enlighten the rest of the world on the same. The secretary of animal husbandry had just returned from Australia with a fascination for sheep and the production of merino wool. Having spent time in a ger in Mongolia, the foreign secretary felt he had discovered the answer to India's housing shortage. Being well trained in gentlemanly virtues, they did not interrupt when one of their brother officers was holding forth. This meant long meetings and few conclusions.

I.K. Gujral, who had plenty of time and no shortage of opinions on his hands, decided that the subcommittees were not adequate fora for the expression of his views, and chose to spend his days in my office. I had no choice but to listen.

Being the low man on the totem pole (remember that these were secretaries that I, a mere joint secretary, was dealing with) meant that there was little I could do other than call the meeting to order and take down the minutes. I could not shepherd the discussion along or goad the eminences grises towards actionable conclusions.

The days ticked by. That blasted goat, Sikander, was making my life miserable. Having heard nothing from our end, Shah had unilaterally decided to bring Sikander along in his plane. Two goatherds – from Baltistan, naturally – would accompany Sikander and brief our chaps on the care and feeding of Baltistani goats.

An additional headache. Were these chaps spies?

Grassing on one's brother officers to one's political masters was a no-no. So the Old Man went on his way unaware of the storm Sikander had raised. I ground my teeth, pulled my hair, engaged in primal scream therapy, and prayed to Parthasarathy Swami.

He took his time, but God finally deigned to acknowledge my fervent outpourings. The outlines of a response to Shah's Sikander poser took shape. There was unanimity on no point. My junior status notwithstanding, I was forced to cast the deciding vote on numerous occasions and each decision occasioned considerable heartburn among those who had been outvoted. I made powerful enemies, but

I knew I had truth, justice and the Indian way of life on my side.

In essence, what was decided was this:

1. We would accept the goat.
2. The goat would go through a machine capable of detecting items such as drugs, communications equipment, nuclear weapons and any other sensitive items that might have been hidden in its stomach.
3. We would send our goatherds (2 numbers) to Islamabad to accompany the goat back to New Delhi.
4. The goat would be renamed Prithviraj Chauhan.
5. Keeping in mind the principle of reciprocity that governs our relations with SAARC countries, we would present a goat to PM Shah during his stay in Delhi. The breed and provenance of the said goat would be decided in due course. Preference would be given to Kashmiri goats.
6. Formal gifting of the goat to take place during the test match.
7. Doordarshan would be given exclusive rights to film the ceremony and the feed would be provided to interested private news channels on payment of a deposit of Rs 50 lakh and a broadcasting fee of Rs 1 crore.

All in all, it was a satisfactory compromise and I had the satisfaction of knowing that India's interests had not been compromised.

11

Sundry Matters

1

'Swami,' called the Old Man. 'Come in here.' There was a quaver in his voice that I knew meant trouble.

The external affairs minister was there along with his secretary and both sported expressions that meant trouble. I seated myself and waited for the storm to break.

'Listen to what he has to say,' said the Old Man, gesturing at his minister.

This worthy had lived up to his title by visiting countries at the rate of one a week. At last count, he had notched up eighty-one visits and it had not taken observers long to note the marked partiality he exhibited towards the US and Western Europe.

The US ambassador had dropped by one morning with a cease and desist request: The State Department was feeling the strain after his eighteenth visit. As a result, Western Europe ended up as unwilling hosts much more often than they would have liked.

Frequency apart, the fact that this worthy spoke only Bhojpuri and ate only food from his native Uttar Pradesh meant that his entourage included cooks and translators, in addition to everything else. Given that he was a politically important member of the GNC, there was little the Old Man could do to curb his peregrinations.

Oh, I forgot to mention that his knowledge of geography and world affairs was confined to his village and the neighbouring districts.

The minister, therefore, gestured at his secretary, who, as secretaries are wont to do, cleared his throat, shuffled the papers he had with him and looked significantly at each of us in turn before speaking. I noticed that the Old Man had shut his eyes.

'The problem, or question, depending on how one chooses to define it, is one of protocol. Since this is, technically speaking, a private visit, it is not, diplomatically speaking, advisable on a matter of principle to accord the visiting delegation the full panoply of an official reception, by which I mean of course the due diplomatic courtesies normally due to a visiting dignitary of this stature as defined by past precedents and reciprocal diplomatic arrangements. In view of this and in view of the unprecedented nature of the visit, which falls outside the ambit of official procedures covered under the protocols agreed to under the Geneva Conventions covering normal reciprocal diplomatic activity between two states not in a formal state of war, guidance is required from the initiator of this particular non-diplomatic interchange and exchange regarding the appropriate arrangements to be made.'

The Old Man opened one eye. 'What did he just say, Swami?'

'Sir, he said that the problem, or question, depending on how one chooses to define it, is one of protocol. Since this is, technically speaking, a private visit, it is not, diplomatically speaking, advisable on a matter of principle to accord the visiting delegation the full panoply of an official reception, by which he meant of course the due diplomatic courtesies normally due to a visiting dignitary of this stature as defined by past precedents and reciprocal diplomatic arrangements. In view of this and in view of the unprecedented nature of the visit, which falls outside the ambit of official procedures covered under the protocols agreed to under the Geneva Conventions covering normal reciprocal diplomatic activity between two states not in a formal state of war, guidance is required from the initiator of this particular non-diplomatic interchange and exchange regarding the appropriate arrangements to be made.'

The Old Man took several deep breaths. 'I know he said that. What did he mean when he said that?'

'I'm not sure, sir.'

'Neither am I.' He turned to his minister. 'What are you and your secretary trying to tell me?'

The minister gestured at his secretary.

The secretary looked embarrassed, shrugged his shoulders and gestured at his minister. Both looked embarrassed and looked down at the floor. The secretary finally spoke:

'In view of the nature of this visit, it is not possible for the external affairs ministry to be represented at the Indira Gandhi International Airport when the Prime Minister of Pakistan arrives. It would be a violation of diplomatic norms.'

'I see,' said the Old Man. 'And who should be at the airport to greet my Pakistani counterpart?'

Once again both stared at the floor before the secretary piped up. 'Since he is your guest, you should, sir.'

I have to say that the Old Man took this remarkably well. No apoplectic fit, no unmanageable rage, just a very knowing nod. 'What is your name?'

The foreign secretary looked shocked. 'Mine, sir?'

'Yes, of course.'

'Gupta, sir. S.C. Gupta.' Known behind his back as Toad on account of his appearance, I should add.

'Gupta, go home and pack your bags. I am sending you to Mogadishu.'

'For what purpose, sir?'

'As our ambassador.'

Toad looked fit to explode with rage and outrage. 'Me? As ambassador? To Mogadishu?'

'Yes,' said the Old Man blandly.

'I'm afraid that you are labouring under a misapprehension, sir. I am the foreign secretary. I cannot be posted as ambassador to a Grade 3 country.'

'Says who?' replied the Old Man.

'It is all spelt out in the Handbook of Diplomatic Procedure. Besides which there is a procedural problem. India is already represented in Mogadishu. Mr Vikram Kapoor was posted there very recently.'

'Gupta, you can take your handbook with you to Mogadishu. I'm sure you'll have plenty of time to read it. I can post you wherever I want. You are going to Mogadishu with the rank of ambassador to look after NRI interests there. Just like the BJP did in Washington DC. Now get out.'

I had never seen the Old Man so angry. There wasn't a hint of it in his appearance, but I knew him well enough to know that he was seething at the effrontery of the Bhojpuri duo.

He turned to his minister. 'You are going to receive Shah at the airport. And remember, there is a goat you are going to have to receive as well.'

2

The minister left and the Old Man turned to me with a satisfied look. 'Good thing you got Tamil Nadu and Chhattisgarh on our side. Now I can kick people's arses a bit.'

I felt good. The Old Man has often been accused of inaction, of standing by when strong leadership was called for, of blandly ignoring the foibles and peccadilloes of his one hundred and seventy-six cabinet colleagues. He had been called senile, a relic and worse. Some had gone so far as to suggest that he might even qualify as the worst PM India has ever had.

Preposterous!

His accusers have no idea of the exigencies involved in managing the GNC, of the cut and thrust of politics at this rarefied level, of the necessary compromises of government. It is all very well to criticize, but how many would have made the personal sacrifices that this eighty-two year old had in the cause of a better and more prosperous nation?

Now I had eased the path a little, allowed him some room for manoeuvre, and he had responded with firmness and a sense of purpose that would have left his critics well short of breath.

Reason enough to feel good.

3

It was getting on to be evening, the wheels of government were engaging smoothly, and I was enjoying a cappuccino with some pastries that the folks at the Taj had sent over.

There is usually a moment in one's day when one can sit back and savour one's existence. Sartre made a lot of this existence business, but even he could not have fully comprehended that unusual concatenation of events and circumstances that led to the feeling of satisfaction, of being at ease with one's world even as one stood poised in the eye of the maelstrom that was the PMO.

For starters, take that cappuccino and those pastries. I can recall a time when khadi and HMT ruled, when the appearance of poverty was almost as important as poverty itself, when people aspired to a bicycle. The privations we were forced to put up with – travel in non-AC trains, watery tea, shared offices (non-AC) with rickety furniture and uncarpeted floors. It is a wonder that we were able to attend to the nation's business with the efficiency that has become a byword in bureaucratic circles worldwide. But we did. And it is only just that we get to savour some of those rewards that the rest of the country today takes for granted.

Yes, life was satisfying. I leaned back, enjoying the view across the lawns, conducting a quiet philosophical soliloquy (refer back to the previous para).

The phone rang.

I must mention here that while life had its share of rewards, all was not perfect. As personal secretary to the PM, I had to answer my own telephone. There were reasons for this, good reasons even – the number was a private one, privy only to those who mattered, and those who called would be put off at the thought of talking to a mere telephone operator. They needed to talk to Someone, and I was that Someone. A damned nuisance, but there it was: a sacrifice made for a higher cause.

My reverie, sorry, philosophical soliloquy, interrupted, I answered with ill humour. 'Yes?'

'Swami? Mr Swami?'

'Yes, speaking.'

Clearly long distance, possibly international. I swallowed the pastry and cleared my throat in anticipation.

'Arre yaar, main hoon.'

Damn! A wasted pastry. 'Who is this?'

'What is this who is this? You do not even recognize your old friends?'

Jugal Kishore Hansraj. Clearly, Geneva had yet to smooth the rough edges of our newest ITU delegate.

'Jugal Kishore,' I exclaimed with false bonhomie. 'What a pleasant surprise! I thought you would have picked up a French accent by now.'

'Oh, that my daughter has. Badi kamaaal ki baat hai. I send her to finishing school and now she is not even talking to her Daddy. Putting all make-up and high heels and you know what?'

'What?'

'Boyfriend also.'

'My God!'

'My God, indeed. I am praying, praying and God is not listening.'

I sent up a silent compliment to God for exercising his discretion as far as granting favours was concerned. 'That is too bad, Jugal Kishore. You were concerned about the Punjabi boys in Janakpuri.'

'Arre, I was mad. Those boys are at least going to college.'

'You mean...'

'Bus conductor, yaar. From Africa.'

'My God!' I added my prayers to his. Even he didn't deserve this.

'Yes, yaar, and it is even worse.'

'How could it be worse?'

'He wears earrings, yaar.'

'Jugal Kishore, I can arrange a transfer back to Delhi if that is what you want.'

'No, no, no, no, no. Not that bad. Bibi is very upset, but she will get over it. Maybe they change the conductor. But good banks here, yaar. Very excellent service. Very highly recommended.'

'I am glad to hear that.'

'Now you will be wondering about the reason for this call.'

'Well, yes.'

'One question you had asked me.'

Yes, I had, and I had also given up all hopes of getting an answer once JKH had decamped. 'Yes?'

'I have the answer.'

I tried to stay calm. 'Yes?'

'Very difficult it was, let me tell you.'

'Yes.'

'I told you earlier, the request was in violation of numerous sections of the Act.'

'Act?'

'The Indian Telegraph Act of 1885.'

'Ah... That Act.'

'Yes, that Act.'

There was a pause. I had this feeling that he was angling for a renegotiation of terms. Dirty bastard! I stayed silent, waiting for him to commit himself. It took a moment or two before he cracked under the weight of the silence.

'Yaar, getting people to get information in violation of the Act is very difficult. Much persuasion required.'

'Jugal Kishore, I'm sure you can be most persuasive when you need to be.'

'No, yaar. You are not understanding. Not that sort of persuasion.'

I was being deliberately obtuse, yes, but JKH did not understand the basics of negotiation – that a deal is a deal. Time he learnt a fact or two about life.

'Then what sort of persuasion?'

'Yaar, you are not understanding?'

'No, I am not understanding. In fact, I thought we had an understanding.'

'Now I am not understanding.'

'Jugal Kishore, we had discussed the matter and had come to an agreement.'

'I know, I know. But yaar, some unforeseen expenses have arisen.'

'Jugal Kishore, you are now working for an international organization. Thanks to me.'

'Yes, I am very grateful...'

'Free of taxes. Thanks to me.'

'Yes, yes...'

'With an allowance for housing.'

'All this I know, yaar. But this Swiss finishing school. It is finishing me off. You want the information, it will be a little more. Sorry, can't help it.'

'In that case, I'll pass. You keep the information.'

'No, yaar. All this time and effort and money. We can come to an understanding.'

I thought to myself that I deserved this, having made the decision to deal with the likes of JKH.

'Sorry, Jugal Kishore. A deal is a deal. If you can't keep to it, the deal is off.'

'Yaar, if I tell someone that you had been asking, it might be very difficult.'

Blackmail now, on top of everything else. To think that the evening had been one of such promise! 'Are you threatening me, Jugal Kishore? I thought you were a friend.'

'Of course, we are friends. Old friends. I am only asking for some slight accommodation.'

'Failing which, you will rat on me.'

'All this rat and things I am not understanding.'

'Jugal Kishore, you can either keep up your end of the deal or face the consequences.'

'Yaar, you are not talking like a friend. You also will have consequences.'

'I will call your friends and colleagues and tell them that your daughter is sleeping with an African bus conductor.'

'You can't do that!'

'That is just for starters. I will arrange for a Letter Rogatory to the Swiss authorities asking for details about certain bank accounts you have opened.'

'Yaar, we are friends....'

'I will revoke your appointment and have you posted instead to Mogadishu as advisor to their telephone department.'

'Yaar, please, yaar. That telephone call was from Mogadishu. From number registered in the name of one Vikram Kapoor. Now please don't tell anyone about my daughter.'

The SOB should have known better than to try bargain with an IAS officer. These flunkies from the allied services and worse have these odd dizzy spells when they feel they are up to taking on or replacing the IAS, conveniently forgetting that they had tripped at the earliest – and easiest – hurdle: the competitive exam. I am a fair man though. I'd give JKH six months in Geneva before bringing him back. He could then worry about Punjabi bus conductors instead.

It took a leisurely three-course dinner at the House of Ming to bring me back to my earlier good humour.

4

Neeta was in my office and we were breaking our heads over a serious problem that had arisen.

Some weeks earlier, the cabinet had gone down to Khajuraho for a brainstorming session and a retreat. Ideas and policies could be considered away from the white heat of political pressures and from the baying mob that insisted on calling itself the Press. It was, as most of these events are, a qualified success.

Carting a hundred and seventy-six ministers, their hangers-on and belongings to Delhi proved a taxing logistical exercise. Being VVVIPs, the red carpet had to be rolled out at IGI for the returning dignitaries. All those feet trampling over it had reduced the carpet to tatters. It had been a carpet that had witnessed history. In its current state though, it was unlikely to witness more history. Suitable for Sikander, perhaps, but not for Shah. It had had its day on the tarmac and was now awaiting its fate as a high-powered committee constituted by the cabinet secretary considered its future. It is not for me to make public the committee's deliberations, but I can say unofficially that the National Museum in New Delhi is the most likely repository of this piece of modern Indian history.

The net result was that with Shah's visit looming, there was no carpet to greet him on. Poor Neeta was in a flap. The problem, as always, was time.

Given enough time, the machinery of government could have been set in motion. A committee would have been constituted, meetings arranged, tenders called for, visits to various carpet makers arranged, the Standing Committee of Parliament consulted and, after due deliberation, a decision regarding a new carpet reached. Decisions were best made when the pressure of circumstances was absent. This principle was the bedrock of governance in India and very well it has worked too.

Consider my office, for instance. I, too, had to contend with a worn out carpet when I assumed office. I put in a requisition for a new carpet and in time (time, incidentally, which included a memorable visit to the Wilton Carpet Factory in England that concluded with some excellent beer and a fine lunch at a nearby pub called The Carping Grouse), a new carpet was requisitioned and installed. (Wilton, in case you were wondering. The Old Man liked it so much that he had his office and bedroom recarpeted and later had the same done for his farmhouse near Meerut and his cottage in Kufri.) This took time, but the results were worthwhile.

I suggested temporary repairs to the old rag, but Neeta was implacable. The honour and prestige of the country were in question. Given half a chance, BBC, with its pro-Pakistan bias, would train its cameras on the carpet and there would be much clucking about how things had gone downhill since the Raj. Besides, Shah, sensitive at the best of times, would consider it an insult. Their army, always nutty, might even consider it grounds for a coup, given that the civilian johnny had allowed this insult in full view of the BBC's cameras.

I had to concur: The Old Man wouldn't be pleased to hear that a coup had occurred next door just because we had skimped on the carpet.

I suggested painting the tarmac red. I had seen adverts for this new matte finish paint and, as long as Shah did not arrive in broad daylight, there was a good chance of fooling the public, Shah and the BBC. In fact, I could suggest that twilight was the most auspicious time, something the Old Man would accept, given his preoccupation with his next life and his desire not to be reborn as a cockroach.

No, said Neeta. Too chancy. Besides, Shah was no fool. He would realize that he was walking on tarmac, not carpet. Politicians, like princesses, were sensitive to that sort of thing.

I called up Wilton in England. The top brass were out having a power lunch at the Carping Grouse. Neeta and I twiddled our thumbs and waited. Actually, I wouldn't have minded having a meaningful tête-à-tête with her. She wasn't a bad sort, her looks were more than passable (she had been second runner-up at the Miss LSR contest, something I knew and something she didn't know I knew and which was therefore something I had in reserve for dire emergencies, which the current situation, perilous though it was, clearly wasn't) and she was an officer from a sister service. Bad advice and the superficial attraction of a foreign posting had probably tilted her towards the lesser service, but I didn't hold that against her. I sensed, though, that she had much on her mind and that this wasn't the best time for a meaningful tête-à-tête. I ordered some munchies from the Taj and we munched in companionable silence.

Their long power lunch done, Wilton called back. 'Mr Swami, how delightful! How may we help you?'

'It is a matter of considerable importance, actually. Mr Shah, the Prime Minister of Pakistan is arriving here in New Delhi shortly and we are short of a red carpet to welcome him. We need it urgently and are willing to have it air-freighted out to us.'

'A red carpet? Would that be for your presidential palace?'

'Well, it is called the Rashtrapati Bhawan actually. Technically, it is not a palace. You see, since we abolished privy purses in 1971, we haven't had maharajas. They call themselves maharajas and they refer to their houses as palaces, but that is technically incorrect. The Rashtrapati Bhawan was never a palace even in a technical sense, as it was the residence of the viceroy. He represented royalty, but was not royalty himself, technically speaking...'

'Mr Swami, pardon the interruption. But this carpet you were referring to...'

'Yes. I was coming to that. I'm sorry, I had forgotten that this was an international call. But to get back to what you were saying, the carpet at the Rashtrapati Bhawan is in good condition.'

I looked inquiringly at Neeta and she nodded. The President did not want all and sundry trampling on his carpet and had saved it from the depredations of the one hundred and seventy-six by the simple expedient of having it locked up when they were about.

'The carpet we need,' I added, 'is for use at the airport.'

There was a slight pause. 'Did I hear you say the airport, Mr Swami?'

'Yes. We need it for use when visiting dignitaries get down from their planes. The last one we had is worn out from overuse. In fact, your Queen's Corgi urinated on it once. Was a major task having it dry-cleaned, I tell you. American sanctions were in force and we were forced to send it to Russia, where...'

'Mr Swami, pardon the interruption. Are you suggesting we supply you with a carpet for use on the tarmac?'

'Yes.'

'I'm sorry, Mr Swami. Wilton supplies high quality carpeting for use in residences and palaces. Should you require carpeting for your presidential, ah, residence, we would be delighted to oblige. But your current requirements necessitate your approaching an alternative supplier. Good day, Mr Swami.'

I had meant to inquire about the Carping Grouse and to reminisce about the delightful hours we had spent there, but he had hung up. Poor sod must have had some accountant breathing down his neck and complaining about his international calls. I pitied him.

Our options cupboard looked bare and Neeta was on the verge of tears. The problem with the IFS is that they inhabit some make-believe world and are easily upset by problems you and I take for granted. The IAS officer has been tested in the crucible of the real world, has had to deal with politicians, junior bureaucrats and members of the public who are eloquent about their rights, but don't give a fig for their responsibilities, and is unfazed when confronted by the impossible.

I put my mind to work. Two alternatives suggested themselves. 'Neeta,' I said, 'you have two choices.'

She looked up, hope filling her large eyes. 'Yes, Swami?'

'You could get a coir carpet from Kerala or a jute one from Bengal. Their favourite colour is red, so you shouldn't have a problem getting the right shade.'

'Which would you recommend?'

I remembered the Dilli Haat fiasco and hesitated about recommending one over the other. Both had commie governments, but were from rival factions and only too ready to go to war over the relative merits of jute and coir. Kerala was one up for the moment as a book on coir had won several awards, something Bengali writers on jute had yet to match. A movie on coir had won some awards as well, and now that Satyajit Ray was dead and gone, there was no one left in Bengal to do cinematic justice to jute. It was something they felt keenly about and I wasn't about to rub things in.

Solomon might have paused a moment or two when confronted with a problem like this, but he hadn't the benefit of training at the Mussoorie Academy. I did and I had the answer. 'We buy one of each, Neeta.'

'Which one would we use, then?'

'Use both. Lay them side by side. The Pakistanis will be impressed by the width of the red carpet, and neither the Mallus nor the Bongs will have cause for complaint.'

Neeta's face brightened, but only for a moment. 'There might be a problem, Swami.'

'What problem?'

'Both will want their carpets on the left.'

'It is relative, don't you see? One carpet will be on the left from Shah's viewpoint, the other will be on the left from the Indian viewpoint. So, both are on the left in a manner of speaking.'

Once more her face brightened before doubts crept in. 'What if the reds don't match?'

'We'll have Shah come in at dusk. No one will notice.'

Relief flooded her features. 'Thanks, Swami. You've saved the day.'

Time, at last, for that tête-à-tête.

12

Goatherds

1

You probably recall the Ad Hoc Committee and its recommendations. One in particular concerned goatherds and the decision was to send our goatherds (2 numbers) to Islamabad to befriend and bring back Sikander. This was because we were concerned that the goatherds they planned to send might well be ISI operatives. Our decision had been conveyed through official diplomatic channels. I had anticipated some protest and it was not long in coming.

'Hello?'

'Hello.'

'Is this the Prime Minister's Office?'

'Yes, Swami speaking.'

'One moment, please. Prime Minister Shah on the line.'

I waited.

'Hello? Keshavji?'

'Sir, this is Swami on the line.'

'Oh, hello Swami. Is Keshavji there?'

'Are you declaring war on us, sir?'

'Ah! He is having his mid-morning nap then.'

'I can't confirm or deny that, sir.'

'Never mind. He is an old man. But there is a problem.'

'Can I help, sir?'

There were some, our foreign secretary, for instance, who would have stood on formality and quoted precedent and diplomatic procedures for not dealing with those they deemed their juniors. Shah and I had spoken earlier, we understood each other and he had no hesitation in having me deal with the problem.

He knew that naptime for the Old Man meant that Swami was in charge, even if my official job description did not extend to running the country.

'Swami, it is about these goatherds.'

'What about them, sir?'

'What is the matter? Do you not like our goatherds?'

'I've never met them, so I can't say, sir.'

'No, no, no. What I mean to say is: are you thinking we will send goatherds who do not know their job?'

'We didn't say that at all, sir.'

'These are first-class goatherds, from families who have been goatherds for generations.'

'We don't doubt that, sir.'

'They even sleep with their goats.'

'What?'

'No, no, you are misunderstanding. You Hindus have dirty minds. What I am saying is that when the goats are babies, they keep them with them for warmth. It is very cold in Baltistan in winter.'

'Very touching, sir.'

'No, no. They don't touch the goats like that. You really have dirty minds.'

'Sorry sir, you misunderstood. I said very touching, not that they touch the goats at night. And we Hindus don't have dirty minds.'

'Okay, okay. No need to get upset. The fact is that they are good goatherds.'

'We've already agreed on that, sir.'

'Then why don't you want our goatherds? You think they are spies or something?'

'Not at all, sir.'

'That they are ISI people? You Indians are mad. Everywhere, everyone is an ISI agent. You blame us for all your troubles.'

'Not all our troubles, sir.'

'Some of your troubles, then. So you accept that our goatherds are good Baltistani goatherds and not spies or ISI agents.'

Something had been nagging me all along and I now saw what it was. This was the PM of Pakistan for heaven's sake and he was calling about a couple of goatherds. Either he had nothing better to do or... the obvious conclusion, the only conclusion really, was that the goatherds were not who Shah claimed they were. I needed to tread cautiously.

'I never said that, sir.'

'So we have agreed that I bring the goatherds with me.'

'No, sir.'

'What?'

'We have agreed only that Baltistani goatherds are good goatherds and that they sleep with infant goats in the winter.'

'But if they are good goatherds, what is your problem? You are always creating these problems.'

'Sir, we appreciate your gesture in presenting a rare Baltistani goat and would like to ensure that it is well looked after here in India.'

'Yes, yes...'

'We have consulted a number of animal welfare experts here and they were unanimous in saying that it is essential that the animal bond well with its keeper. Animals lacking this strong bond are apt to suffer trauma and stress and likely to become violent. In view of this, they felt that a period of bonding prior to your bringing the goat here would help it adapt better when it finds itself in surroundings alien to it.'

Silence.

'How can I be sure you are not sending spies?'

'We have more pressing things to do than send spies disguised as goatherds.'

'All the time you are making devious plans to dismember my country.'

'You end up blaming us for all your troubles, sir.'

'Not all, only some. The Americans are responsible for the rest. Off the record, of course.'

'Sir, the goatherds we send can be put up at Islamabad Zoo...'

'Why Islamabad Zoo? What's so special about Islamabad Zoo?'

'Nothing. Why are you getting so worked up? Do you have terrorist camps there, sir?'

'We don't have terrorist camps anywhere in Pakistan. We only support freedom fighters.'

'Then you have freedom fighter camps in Islamabad Zoo?'

'You agree then, on the record, that there are no terrorists, only freedom fighters in Pakistan?'

'Of course not, sir. You've just admitted that you run terrorist training camps in Islamabad Zoo.'

'No, no. No such thing. But you can't be sending your goatherds wherever you please.'

'We are not sending goatherds wherever we please. Only where the goat is. There is only one relevant question, sir. Where is Sikander right now?'

'Where? In Lahore Zoo, I think.'

'Then our goatherds can go there and spend time with him. You can make sure they are guarded and don't leave the premises. Only provide them meals.

If there are camps in Lahore Zoo as well, they can be shut down while the goatherds are there. They needn't even see the other animals.'

'Okay,' he said sulkily. 'Who are the goatherds you are sending?'

'I'll find out and let you know, sir. Shall I tell Mr Motwani you called?'

'No, no. It's all right.'

We hung up.

2

There are times, I must admit, when the machinery of government takes on a life of its own.

Two goatherds, we had said, having in mind nothing more than a couple of goatherds picked up from Patparganj or one of those places across the river where goats abound and who were looking for a free trip to Pakistan. Instead, a copy of the minutes ended up at the Union Public Services Commission. They put out the following advert:

Position: Goatherd (Grade VII)

Numbers: 2 (two)

Salary: Rs 2,800-50-3,200-75-3,600. DA and Bonus as per Central Government Rules. Housing Allowance as per Central Government Rules.

Qualifications: B VSc from a Recognized University with a minimum of 55% (50% for candidates from Scheduled Castes and Scheduled Tribes) and a minimum of five (5) years' experience tending goats. Preference may be given to those with experience in tending mountain goats.

In exceptional cases, viz., those with more than fifteen (15) years experience in tending mountain goats, the marks requirement may be reduced or waived.

Reservations: One (1) post only to be reserved for candidates from Scheduled Castes and Scheduled Tribes.

Age: Candidates should have completed thirty (30) years on 30 June 2004.

Documents to be provided: Copies of degrees and higher secondary school records duly certified by a Gazetted Officer. Proof of Age (Ration Card, Driver's Licence, Passport) to be attached. An Affidavit attested by a Tehsildar, Village Munsif or a Gazetted Officer may be accepted in lieu of the foregoing. Proof of experience in tending goats/ mountain goats, viz., an Affidavit attested by a Gazetted Officer.

All documents to be provided in triplicate.

Seven (7) passport sized photographs to be provided.

Method of Selection: An examination following which shortlisted candidates will be called for an interview. Second class sleeper fare from their domicile (as entered in a valid ration card) to New

Delhi will be provided to candidates shortlisted for the interview.

Additional Information: Only candidates with a valid passport will be considered.

Overkill, you would think, but with mere days to go to the visit (and remember, the goatherds had to be in Lahore Zoo bonding with Sikander a day or two before that), the UPSC had some twenty thousand (20,000) applications for the post, the vast majority from Bihar and all claiming experience with mountain goats.

I am from the Bihar cadre and, while I'm no zoologist, logic suggested that mountain goats were scarce, if not non-existent, in Bihar. Each of the twenty thousand, though, had the attached affidavit attesting to their experience.

The chaps over at the UPSC were in a tizzy. All twenty thousand had made their way to Delhi to sit for the examination. Anticipating only a hundred or so valid applications, they had set aside two smallish halls for the written test. Now there were twenty thousand aspiring goatherds ruining their lawns with paan spittle and groundnut shells. They were also getting restive.

The voice of the caller from the UPSC was shrill with panic. 'Mr Swami! We have an emergency on our hands!'

'What do you mean?'

'This advertisement for goatherds. There are far more applicants than we had anticipated.'

'How many?'

'About twenty thousand.'

'Good Lord!'

'Yes sir. We have also been praying, but the Good Lord has not been listening. They are making a mess outside and now they are all insisting on writing the examination.'

'Tell me something. Whose daft idea was it to put out this ad?'

'What is the meaning of daft, sir?'

'Stupid.'

'Oh. But it is as per our rules and regulations, sir.'

'Rules and regulations? For goatherds?'

'The Government Service Rules of 1960 make an explicit mention of goatherds employed by the Central government and categorizes them as Grade VII, VIII or IX. We have only followed the guidelines laid out therein.'

'And what does your test contain?'

'It is as per the UPSC guidelines. A general knowledge test covering Indian and world history, Indian social studies, basic mathematics...'

'How long is this test?'

'Three hours, sir.'

'For hiring two goatherds? What is wrong with you?'

'We are required to follow rules and regulations, sir.'

'Ask them to draw a goat. Make it a drawing test. We'll draw two winners at random. I'll ask the PM to pick the two winners.'

'Sorry sir, but that would be a violation of the rules. We could be reprimanded by the Comptroller and Auditor General and by the Standing Committee of Parliament. Mr Jha, MP from Jhajha, is chairman of the committee and very particular when it comes to matters concerning his home state. Most of the candidates are from Bihar, sir.'

'Why does a goatherd have to undergo a general knowledge test?'

'The guidelines laid out by the Rules of 1960 are...'

'Okay. I get your point. Why don't you postpone the examination?'

'Technical difficulties, sir.'

'Technical difficulties?'

'Section MCXII, Para 3, Sub-Para 4 read in conjunction with Section XX...'

'In other words, if you postpone, the CAG and Mr Jha will be after your blood.'

'Yes, sir. The conditions laid down for postponement have not been met in toto.'

'What if I ask the Pakistani PM to declare war on us? You can then declare force majeure and cancel the whole bloody thing.'

'Technical difficulties will stand in the way of the proposed course of action, sir.'

'Why?'

'Only the chairman has the authority to declare force majeure, sir.'

'Why can't he, then? I'll get you your war declaration in half an hour. I'll even get Shah to fax a statement to your chairman to that effect. What is his fax number?'

'The chairman is travelling, sir.'

'Where is he?'

'In Rio de Janeiro.'

'What? What is he doing in Rio?'

'He is heading a delegation studying recruitment procedures in Brazil, Argentina and Paraguay.'

This was proving difficult. 'There must be some acting chairman?'

'The entire board is in Rio, sir.'

'The entire board is absent? Can you hold the examination if the entire board is absent? Who is the adjudicating authority then? How can you hold the examination in the absence of a proper adjudicating authority?'

'I'm not sure, sir.'

'Then the whole exercise is mala fide and ultra vires. You can be taken to court by any candidate who feels aggrieved by the outcome of the said mala fide procedure. Mr Jha will also hold an inquiry into the procedural deficiencies therein.'

'What should I do, sir?'

'Postpone it indefinitely. On the grounds I just cited.'

I put the phone down and sent up a prayer of thanks. A wholly avoidable crisis averted. I sent a chaprasi down to the river to get hold of a couple of goatherds before it slipped my mind. Time, then, to move on to more important matters.

3

I had just immersed myself in a file when the UPSC chappie called again. I could hear loud noises in the background and he had to shout to make himself heard.

'The candidates are rioting, sir! They are throwing stones! They are turning violent!'

'Why?'

'They were upset that the examination was postponed, sir.'

'Call the police, then.'

'Technical difficulties, sir. Under the procedures laid down, only the chairman or a duly constituted authority has the authority to call in the police.'

'And all the duly constituted authorities are in Rio?'

'Yes, sir.' There was the sound of a crash. 'They have broken my window, sir. They might damage my air-conditioner, sir. Three years it took for the AC to be installed.' He was close to tears.

Time, yet again, for an on-the-spot decision. 'Tell them you are sending them on a study tour.'

'Study tour?'

'Yes, yes. Study tour to Khajuraho.'

'Khajuraho?'

'Yes, Khajuraho.'

'But how, sir? There are twenty thousand of them.'

'We will charter some trains.'

'But our budget...?'

'The Prime Minister has asked me to spare no efforts to make the Pakistani PM's visit a success. This will be paid for out of funds earmarked for the visit.'

'I will make the announcement immediately, sir.' A pause, then, 'There might be a problem, sir.'

I could hear glass shattering in the background and didn't need him to tell me that there was a problem.

'You've already told me there is a problem. I'm well aware of it. I've already suggested a solution in case you missed hearing it in the din.' I was shouting as well to make sure I was heard.

'Don't shout, sir. Bad for my ears. Too much shouting all the time. The problem is a different one, sir.'

'What?'

'But what will be the subject matter of this study tour? That is the problem. Our rules make it explicit that sanction may be given for study tours only when the subject matter of the said tours thereof is stated clearly and unambiguously in the preamble to the document wherein the details thereof are laid out.'

'Tell them that the details of the study tour will be announced in due course. On second thoughts, tell them that it is to study goat herding techniques as practised during the times of the Chandela dynasty. If there are any other practices of the Chandelas that they wish to pursue, that is their headache.'

'One minute, sir, I am writing all this down. One minute. How do you spell Chandela? And headache?'

4

Riots on the Banks of the Yamuna
By Our Correspondent

New Delhi: Traffic on the bridges connecting New Delhi to Noida and other trans-Yamuna areas was repeatedly disrupted when riots on the banks of the river spilled over onto the bridges and surrounding streets.

The problem evidently arose when an official, allegedly from the PMO, went to the area to hire two goatherds. Unable to decide amongst themselves, the goatherds sought time to decide the identity of the two to be hired. Time proved no balm as the dispute degenerated into one involving goatherds from Western Bihar pitted against those from Eastern UP.

The former soon found themselves outnumbered as a politician based in Ghaziabad brought in some goons to support the latter.

Upset at the lack of civic amenities despite repeated promises by politicians, a group hailing from Haryana, hitherto aloof from the dispute, turned on the politician. Matters took on an ugly turn when a Tata Safari car owned by the politician was set on fire.

An attempt by the Delhi Police to calm matters by resorting to a mild lathi charge, accompanied by warning shots fired into the air, only exacerbated matters. Weapons, including country rifles, bombs and an AK-47 rifle, were brought into play. The army was summoned to quell the disturbance. A tense calm was finally restored after a standoff lasting three hours. Estimates of casualties vary from the official two dead and eight injured to the goatherds' claim of one hundred and seventy-three dead and four hundred and eighty injured.

Contacted late in the evening, the PMO denied that it had sought to hire two goatherds. A commission of inquiry headed by a retired Supreme Court

judge has been ordered to look into
the incident. A solatium for those
killed and injured in the incident
has been announced.

5

Net result: no goatherds.

I needed to get back to Shah about the goatherds.
No doubt the ISI and the generals were after him
to ensure that the two were not spies or anything
like that. Trust them not to trust us.

Inspiration, unaccountably absent for a while,
returned: I had just the goatherds I needed. A mite
short on goat tending experience, yes, and more than
likely not to welcome the offer with open arms.

The two men from Mogadishu: Vikram Kapoor
and Toad. That inappropriate telephone call from
one and that inappropriate suggestion from the other
(remember he wanted the Old Man to trek down to
IGI) would ensure compliance in case either chose
to fuss. And yes, I must admit that the thought of
the two spending time in Lahore Zoo was hugely
satisfying.

13

Shah Arrives

1

There are moments when a feeling of satisfaction at a job well done overwhelms you, when a sense of light-headedness or giddiness takes over, when the long hard slog that got you to this point is momentarily forgotten.

This was one.

We had assembled at IGI to welcome Shah and his entourage. The IFS, regrettably, was absent: They had chosen this most inappropriate moment to go on a mass casual leave to protest Kapoor and Toad's latest assignment. I've always wondered about their tendency to put petty personal matters above national interest. It is in this regard, I think, that we differ most from them. How typical, how thoughtless of them to attempt to sabotage what was likely to be the most significant visit to our shores by a foreign dignitary. (Some might be inclined to grant this accolade to Alexander of Macedonia. His visit was not in response to an official invitation, however, and does not, as a result, qualify as a significant visit.)

They had reckoned without us, however. The IAS had stepped into the breach and we had burned the midnight oil to soothe any diplomatic feathers that might have been inadvertently ruffled as the fine points of protocol were haggled over. As always, I was astonished at the tendency of diplomatic feathers to get ruffled by the slightest of provocations. It was almost as though they deliberately allowed their feathers to get ruffled in order to justify their existence. Perhaps I needed to put up a note to the Old Man suggesting the abolition of the IFS. Keeping in mind national interest, of course.

There was a crowd gathered on the runway and a buzz of chitchat and gossip wound its way up into the cool, clear dusk. A good number of the cabinet were present: I had ensured that those unable to find a place on the sofa were here to shake Shah's hand in person. The foreign minister, earlier protestations notwithstanding, was there: He enjoyed his job and wanted to keep it. Fazlur Rehman was there, as were a scattering of diplomats. The machine that was to ensure that Sikander was filled with entrails rather than explosives stood off to one side. A long line of limousines stood by to whisk the VVVIPs to their suite at the Maurya. Security was discreet

but tight: The Press – bar the Doordarshan crew –
were cordoned off in a distant hangar to prevent
their foolish questions, which always marred the
solemnity of these events.

Shah's plane flew low overhead, then landed.
The ladder, decked with jasmine, was wheeled out,
Shah stepped out into the glare of the floodlights,
the band struck up the national anthem. He smiled
and waved for Doordarshan's benefit, then stepped
down the ladder, followed the prescribed three steps
later by his begum.

2

I was waiting at the foot of the steps to greet him
on behalf of the Old Man and the People of India,
when there was this commotion behind him. Shah
had barely time to turn and see what was going on
when a blur flew down the steps, knocking down
first his begum and then him.

Next in line was yours truly. As I was knocked off
my feet, I realized that the blur was something I had
seen a few days earlier. Something that had marred
the solemnity of that occasion as well – Sikander.
His head was down, his horns primed for action,
and he looked annoyed. He charged off across
the tarmac, scattering the gathered dignitaries. He
looked happy to be free from confinement.

I looked back. Shah had ended up in a heap a
foot or so from where I lay.

'On behalf of Mr Motwani and the People of India, I welcome you to India, sir. Are you all right?'

He got up gingerly and dusted himself off before shaking his head. 'Bloody goat!' he said finally.

'Where are the goatherds, sir?'

Kapoor and Toad were supposed to ensure that this sort of thing didn't happen. They were not professional goatherds, true, but they had had a day or two to establish a rapport with Sikander.

'Your bloody goatherds have gone on strike.'

'What?'

'In solidarity with their colleagues, so they say. Do goatherds regularly go on strike in your country?'

'No, sir. Where are they right now?'

'In the plane, the damn fools, squatting on the floor.'

'Do I have your permission to arrest them, sir?'

'They are your goatherds. Why do you need my permission?'

'Technically they are on Pakistani soil, sir.'

'Oh. Do you want me to arrest them for you?'

'If you don't mind, sir.'

'No problem. I've never met such arrogant goatherds in my life. Pompous fools. They wanted mutton biryani served to them.'

'I hope you turned down the request, sir.'

'Of course. Can't have goatherds getting too big for their boots. Speaking of which, they had Bally shoes, which they must have stolen from somewhere.

I had them searched and found Marks and Spencer underwear, shirts and pants from Harrods and blazers from Carnaby Street. Hardly what you expect goatherds to wear, so we confiscated the lot. Hope you don't mind. They are your goatherds after all.'

'Not at all, sir. But I hope they have some clothes on.'

'They wouldn't wear the clothes we gave them, but we made it clear that it was either those clothes or no clothes. So they agreed to wear the clothes we gave them. Another thing. They insisted on using toilet paper. Funny goatherds you sent us.'

'Hmm, yes. I must look into how they were selected. Will they stay on the plane after you arrest them, sir?'

'Well, the plane will be here for a few days. Might need to have it fumigated if these goatherds are on board all the time. You see, the clothes we gave them were those of the camel-keeper at the Lahore Zoo.'

'We could lodge them temporarily in Tihar Jail. You can take them back when you leave.'

'Good idea. Now what are you going to do about Sikander?'

I looked around. The ministers and the diplomatic riffraff were getting impatient. They wanted the introductions done and finished with so that they could get back to their mistresses and cocktail parties.

There was an important-looking cop standing by. 'Where is the goat?' I asked him.

He pointed to a distant part of the runway where some fleetly moving figures could be seen. 'Minister sahib has gone chasing the goat, sir.'

'Minister sahib?'

'Foreign minister sahib. Some policemen are helping him.'

I knew he wanted to keep his job, but this was a bit much. Even so, I had little choice, but to let him go chasing after Sikander. I had on a suit and tie and, besides, he had too much of a head start. I turned to Shah:

'Sikander will be taken care of, sir. In the meanwhile, might I introduce you to the dignitaries who have gathered here to greet you?'

'Good. I hope you are not planning to have him for biryani. He is a rare goat.'

'We have a cage prepared for him at the Delhi Zoo, sir. I'm sure there will be many visitors to see this symbol of friendship between our countries.'

Sikander was eventually captured. Our foreign minister had tended goats as a youth, it turned out, and knew a thing or two about catching goats that had gone runabout. It required the efforts of seventeen cops to force Sikander through the machine. Happily, he was clean; unhappily, the machine was damaged beyond repair. One more item added to the burgeoning list of expenses.

3

MPs Walk Out Following Uproar over Scenes at Airport
By Our Correspondent

New Delhi: Parliament was plunged into chaos yesterday when MPs cutting across party lines denounced the unruly scenes at IGI Airport consequent to the arrival of the Prime Minister of Pakistan.

Led by Mrs Kumudben Shah, MPs from the Opposition were on their feet denouncing what they said was Pakistan's attempt to deliberately insult India in full view of the international media. Mrs Shah went on to add that she was ashamed to bear the same surname as the Pakistani Premier, and was contemplating changing it. This was greeted by thumping of desks.

A member's private motion to require all Indians named Shah to change their name was disallowed by the Speaker. Following agitated protests by members who stormed the well of the House, a recess was called. An all-party conference held in the Speaker's chambers resolved to constitute a parliamentary committee to study the suggestion.

Reconvening later in the evening, agitated members sought the cancellation of the test series. Other members expressed sympathy for the Prime Minister's representative, Mr Swami, whose buttocks were bruised when the runaway goat butted him. The role played by the foreign minister in capturing the runaway goat came in for appreciative mention. A section of the House advocated killing the goat and feeding it to the poor. This suggestion was met with a volley of protests by members belonging to the BJP, who spoke up for vegetarianism and wanted the goat returned to Pakistan.

The session ended with the foreign minister assuring the members that suitable diplomatic measures were being considered and that the Prime Minister would address the members and their concerns the next day.

'Why are these people agitating like this? Mr Swami himself welcomed me to India and mentioned nothing about this injury to his buttocks. In fact, I too was knocked down by the goat, as was my wife. Are these people suggesting that we did this deliberately? As for Mr Swami, if he so wishes, I will summon my personal physician, Dr Pathan, from Peshawar to examine his buttocks. And the goat running away like that – it is not our fault. The goatherds sent by your government went on strike. In fact, they were supposed to be travelling with Sikander, the goat, in the luggage section of the plane. They insisted on travelling with the other passengers and that is why Sikander travelled in the passenger section. And after this, they go on strike. Badi ajeeb baat hai, aur uske baad we get blamed for all this. Go ask your goatherds why they went on strike. They are in Tihar Jail, I am told, go ask them.'

Shah was the very picture of an aggrieved Prime Minister. I switched off the TV and turned to the Old Man. 'Sir, I don't want some Pathan doctor poking around my you-know-what.'

'What is your you-know-what?' replied the Old Man with a knowing leer.

I changed the subject. 'What should we do about... about the... goatherds?'

'Who are these goatherds anyway?'

I had hoped it wouldn't come to this. You see, I hadn't told the Old Man that I had yanked Toad and Kapoor from their Mogadishu sinecure and sent them along to Lahore Zoo. I realized now that Machiavelli had nothing on IFS officers when it came to deviousness. They had turned a regulation punishment posting on its head and were threatening an IAS preserve. I had no doubt that reporters were heading to Tihar Jail even as I pondered the alternatives. I needed to head them off at the pass.

'The goatherds? I wouldn't know, sir.'

Damn! I had to cut this conversation off at the pass as well. Why the hell did Shah have to mention that they were in Tihar Jail?

'Funny thing, this. You know, I am eighty-two years old.'

Oh shit! This had the sound of a longwinded reminiscence.

'I've seen plenty of things in this long life of mine,' he went on. I continued to fidget and hoped it wouldn't show. Damn! 'I've seen Gandhiji, have I ever told you that?'

Another day, another time and I would have been happy to listen to him ramble on about Gandhiji. Not now. 'Yes, sir. You've told me about it.'

'Which one? The meeting at Sabarmati, the meeting in Wardha or the one in Delhi?'

'All three, sir.'

'That cannot be. In fact, I've told nobody about the time I saw him in Sabarmati. For many years, I was embarrassed about it. But now I am eighty-two years old and it doesn't really matter. In a few months, I will have retired and be meditating in Rishikesh. With Sri Sri Sri Guruji. A very wise man. You have met him, spoken to him. Did you not feel the peace, the serenity that surrounds him?'

'Yes, sir,' I lied.

'There are many mistakes we make in our lives. Even I have made such mistakes.'

I was mentally calculating how long it would take to get from the Maurya to Tihar Jail. I glanced at my watch; I hadn't much time.

'Excuse me, sir,' I interrupted.

'Yes, bete?'

'Bathroom, sir.'

'One or two?'

'Two, sir.'

'You'd better see a doctor. Too many twos you are doing. Anyway, carry on. I'll wait for you.'

4

'I'm calling from the PMO. Under no circumstances is the Press to meet the goatherds.'

'One moment, sir.'

The moment stretched on. The Old Man would be waiting and would doubtless have something to say about the time I took over my two. Bloody embarrassing, but there was nothing I could do about it. Shit! Couldn't the SOB answer the telephone?

'Sir?'

'Yes?'

'Superintendent sahib has gone home.'

'Yes, yes, I understand. But I am telling you... the goatherds...'

'Which goatherds?'

'How many goatherds do you have there?'

'There was some problem near the river. Lots of goatherds were arrested. They are still here and refusing to take bail.'

'What?'

'You see, sahib, we are having some computer classes for the inmates. Now they all want to learn the computer. At sarkari expense.'

'Let them learn. I'm not bothered about them. Don't you remember the two goatherds who came with the Pakistani Prime Minister?'

'One moment, sir.'

More minutes dragged by. I squirmed and seethed and cursed. Didn't the bastard realize that this was urgent?

'Sir?' Back on the line and about bloody time, too. 'You are referring to Kapoor and Gupta?'

'Yes, yes.'

'They've escaped, sir.'

'What?'

'They disguised themselves as IFS officers and walked out. They fooled the guards completely.'

'I don't believe this.'

'An inquiry is under way, sir. Superintendent sahib can explain. But he has gone home and will be available only tomorrow. About eleven o'clock.'

'Fifteen minutes. Swami, you have a problem. I am calling an ambulance.'

'I am okay, sir,' I said weakly.

'No, you're not. You can't go on working in the condition you are in. Now go lie down while I send for the ambulance.'

14

Bum Times

1

Humiliation. Utter embarrassment. By now, most of Delhi knew that Sikander had butted me in the course of his wanderings at IGI. And when the ambulance drew up at the All India Institute of Medical Sciences, an ambulance that had been summoned by the Old Man himself, there was quite a reception committee, starting with the director of the institute, along with assorted flunkies, a gaggle of doctors and nurses and including what looked like all the Class III and Class IV employees of the institute. The TV news crews, tipped off by someone or the other, were there as well, recording the event for posterity.

In view of the earlier news reports, they all assumed that my posterior was responsible for this urgent and unscheduled dash to the hospital. The director held forth on the line of treatment he proposed to follow and went on to add that I might have difficulty sitting down for a week or two thereafter. There were many clucks of sympathy at this and my protestations that this was all a big misunderstanding and that there was nothing the matter with me were ignored. Some of the TV guys wanted a close-up of the injured posterior and it took a not immoderate display of violence on my part to hang on to my pants and my dignity.

Things were not much better in my room. My bruised derriere had acquired a status akin to that of the Kohinoor diamond and everyone – doctors, nurses and chaprasis – came to have a peek. Listening to the nurses' poor-dears and oh-dears was almost as annoying as having a group of frowning doctors poking around with unsterilized fingers and ballpoint pens. There was nothing I could do about this. Each time I insisted that I was completely all right, that I had work I needed to get back to, there were murmurs about how brave I was and how I was setting an exemplary example by my devotion to duty.

A delegation of MPs led by Kumudben Shah came to visit and reacted much the same way.

Later that day, Ms Shah showed up on TV. Tears flowed down her face as she recounted the tale of my bravery and devotion to duty. I thought I would puke: It seemed only a matter of time before I was accorded the same status as the Kargil martyrs, maybe even a beatification by the Vatican.

The Old Man himself came by and advised me good rest. He also took the opportunity to examine the bathroom and pronounced himself satisfied. I wasn't, but good sense and protocol meant that I couldn't voice my complaints in the glare of the visiting TV crews.

All the while, I had this nagging feeling that something wasn't quite right. There was something fishy about the way I had been bundled off to the hospital, about the way I was being tested, poked and prodded for what was, after all, a mere bruise. There was something about the whole episode that felt like some monstrous practical joke; it was as though everyone was just waiting for some cue to burst into laughter. I broke my head over it, to no avail. I was grounded, and the world hurtled on to some uncertain future.

2

Neeta dropped in one morning and gazed at me sorrowfully. I was fed up with my life; I was fed up with visitors; I was in no mood for banter.

I stared fixedly at the wall and sulked.

'You don't know when to stop, do you?'

I wasn't about to dignify the conversation with an answer.

'We are all used to a certain amount of backbiting, a certain amount of manipulation. You went too far.'

I felt a pricking of interest, but wasn't going to show my interest just yet. Good negotiating tactics. Besides, I was annoyed with her. She, of all people, should have put national interest ahead of the petty concerns of her service and refrained from joining the others in going on casual leave. Her unexpected absence had meant an added emergency or two for me. I had dealt with them, but they were two episodes I would rather not have had crop up.

'You know, you've made some pretty serious enemies. Even Motwani will not take on the foreign service for your sake.'

What was she talking about?

'You know, you should have been sacked. This is just a compromise.'

'What is just a compromise?' I blurted out.

'Your being kept here in the hospital.'

There. Now I knew that my suspicions were not without reason. 'Why am I being kept here?'

'Sending them to Mogadishu, well, I suppose you could have got away with that. But this business of packing them off to Lahore... Gupta was very attached to that blazer. He is still upset when anyone mentions it.'

'You mean Gupta and Kapoor are behind this... this... this outrage?'

'Outrage is a very strong term, Swami. You are, after all, in a VVVIP room, your food is being catered by the Taj – there are any number of people who would give an arm and a leg to be in your position.'

'Name one.'

'Me.'

'Oh. Anyway. What is that bastard Kapoor up to?'

'I wish you wouldn't refer to him as a bastard. He was rather sweet over dinner last night.'

'What? You had dinner with him? Have you taken leave of your senses?'

'I was hoping I could talk sense into you. You are, after all, like a brother to me. Anyway, he was right. You have lost it. Hopefully, only temporarily. Vikram, by the way, is now in your old job at the PMO. Very busy with tomorrow's test match. He said to say hi. See you, Swami. Get well soon.'

3

I cannot do verbal justice to the feelings that seethed and raged within me after Neeta left. Had I been Krakatoa, I would have exploded. I wasn't. I was an IAS officer and IAS officers don't explode like mere volcanoes.

I am also human, though, and I have to say that my feelings had the better of me for long moments.

Not for too long, though. You know the old adage about a crisis making a man? That was my situation. I had been trapped in an invidious, insidious conspiracy; defeat and disgrace stared me in the face; I could almost hear the chortles rising up from the external affairs ministry, but I wasn't about to throw in the towel.

Time, then, to crank up the grey cells, with a fervent prayer to Sri Parthasarathy Swami to help things along. A moment's reflection and I saw where I had gone wrong. I should not have sent them to Tihar – place leaked like an Indian umbrella. I remembered now how Charles Sobhraj had made it a habit almost of breaking out of the place. Having got out, they had been able to manipulate things to their advantage. There was no reason why I could not do what they had done.

I knew the routine of the place and I waited for that hour when the tea break depleted the nursing staff to negligible numbers and the corridors were clear. Thankfully, my clothes still hung in the wardrobe. I changed and walked out.

I had made it as far as the main gate when I was stopped by some security types. 'Who are you, sahib?' asked one.

'An IFS officer,' I replied, unthinkingly. I must have had Toad and Kapoor on my mind.

He looked me up and down. 'Nahin sahib, you are not an IFS officer.'

'What do you think I am, then?'

'You look like an IAS officer, sahib.'

I was too flabbergasted to respond or to object when he steered me back to the admissions desk to get an Out pass.

You can guess the rest: I was back in my room before I could say Raghupati Raghav Raja Ram. I did have a moment when I asked the security type how he knew I was IAS and not IFS.

'You were on TV, sahib,' he said with a smile.

4

Damn! I had thought this was going to be easy, and all I had done was put everyone on their guard. The nurses peeked in every few minutes now, the doctors tut-tutted and told me not to strain myself overly. They merely shook their heads when I pointed out that I was doing precisely nothing and, therefore, could not possibly be straining myself. In the few minutes I had to myself before the nurses peeked in again, I tried to make sense of this – without success.

One of the nurses was a Malayali and I figured I stood a better chance with her. Solidarity of the Southies against Toad, Kapoor and the forces of evil, if you get my drift. And in case your thoughts begin drifting after having got my drift, I should mention that Mary was a Christian and, as such, a practising Iyengar like me would harbour no untoward feelings towards her. She was pretty, I admit, and the dimple when she smiled more than slightly distracting. But that was all in the realm of the abstract. Call it feeling, Cubist style.

Anyway, I tried my Malayalam on her, wanting to know just why I was being detained in the hospital. She broke into giggles. An attempt on my part to clarify matters only precipitated a further volley of giggles, which threatened to get out of control. There was little to do but wait until communication was restored.

What she said was this: overwork had rendered unstable my mental equilibrium. In other words, I was supposed to be a lunatic and the staff were to treat me as such. There was a fresh burst of giggles as she left the room.

I was left pondering my fate and the propensity of Malayali nurses to giggle at the least provocation.

5

It rained that night – unseasonal rains that reflected the dank depths to which my feelings had sunk.

Shah was hosting a banquet and some overexcited commentator on TV gushed forth every time he spotted a celebrity. He made me sick. I could see Vikram Kapoor looking and acting busy and generally making out as though he was the lynchpin holding this whorl of events together. He made me sick. Pan to the dining area where the Old Man and Shah sat at a table set on the stage, beaming benevolently down on the masses. They made me sick. And the masses themselves, gaudily painted and bejewelled and decked in the best of designer fashion, they made me sick as well.

Nevertheless, there was something about the spectacle that kept me glued to it – sort of like watching something nasty with a horrified, but irresistible fascination. There was something gross about the way they ate in full glare of the cameras. A trickle of gravy dribbled down the Old Man's chin and Shah burped up some soup onto his napkin. What was Kapoor thinking? I would never have let the TV crews in while the Old Man ate; there are some things best done in private. You cannot, after all, expect an eighty-two- year-old to handle his cutlery with the finesse of a Doon School graduate. But that fool Kapoor seemed to have got it into his thick skull that exposure and more exposure was what the Old Man craved.

Food, drink and speeches done with, they made their way out. Shah's limousine drew up and I sat up. This was a major breach of protocol. Shah was the host and, even if he did not wish to waste his time seeing off the glitterati, he should have waited for the Old Man to leave before summoning his limousine. Common sense really, the sort of thing you are expected to know before entering Mussoorie. What on earth was Kapoor up to? He was nowhere to be seen and it struck me that he was probably still in the dining hall gobbling the last of the jalebis. Gross dereliction of duty, the sort of thing I would have never countenanced.

There was some conversation between the PMs and, horror of horrors, the Old Man got into Shah's limo!

A minor matter, you may think, but an enormous violation of all diplomatic norms and not something any self-respecting personal secretary would have allowed. A word or two of explanation is in order here. Shah's limo, technically speaking, was Pakistani territory. The Old Man should never have been allowed in without due security and the necessary diplomatic groundwork. Damn it, he would not even have had his diplomatic passport with him. Shah could arrest him, kill him even and there was nothing the Republic of India could do about it. We would be the laughing stock of the world. That sneaky bastard Shah had taken advantage of my absence to pull a fast one on us.

My blood boiled. Our national interests were being frittered away and here I was, unable to do anything about it. I peeked out into the corridor: The nurses were there all right. One saw me and motioned me back into my room with a stern shake of her head. There was no sign of the giggly Miss Mary.

I was in a difficult predicament. I had been labelled a loony (okay, stressed out from overwork, which is saying much the same thing) and no one was likely to take me seriously. It was more likely that they would assume I had lost all my remaining marbles and disregard anything I said. I thought hard and something *did* occur to me.

Kumudben Shah.

She had been sympathetic, she had made the right noises, she had even threatened to change her name. Not the most obvious of choices, I admit, but I hadn't the luxury of choice. I called her.

She was an MP and MPs are not generally receptive to calls from bureaucrats admitted to hospital on account of stress. I persevered, though, and finally got through. I explained the situation.

I should mention here that Kumudben was no chum of the Old Man. She was a tough one and had been elected as an independent. The Old Man had rebuffed her feelers when it came to the cabinet. Adding Kumudben to his one hundred and seventy-six malcontents made little sense to him, but she didn't see things the same way and had been a thorn in his side ever since.

She heard me out noncommittally.

I had done what I could. Now I could only lie down and wait.

6

Kumudben did not let me down.

It must have been past eleven when we spoke. By six the next morning, she was hogging all the headlines. There was a major demonstration going on outside the Pakistan high commission, another one at the Maurya where Shah was staying, and a third outside the Kotla stadium. The theme was the same – the insult to the Indian PM and the consequent demand that Shah return to Islamabad along with his cricket team. A satisfactory level of noise was being generated.

Kumudben herself was on TV. Indignation poured forth. India was a hospitable country, but hospitality had its limits. Pakistan in the person of Shah had crossed those limits. Ergo, they didn't deserve our hospitality and friendship. Deceit and gamesmanship were their stock in trade. We should not have let ourselves be taken in by those self-serving, duplicitous so-and-sos. There was more along similar lines, all delivered in that shrill and angry tone that was Kumudben's stock in trade.

The Pakistanis were probably in shock, or else they hadn't recovered from the banquet. There was no one to counter this flow of vitriol. No one from External Affairs or the PMO either. Kumudben had the field all to herself.

Over at Kotla, there was another problem brewing. This hadn't the makings of a disaster yet and so occupied a distant second place to Kumudben. The sofa, yes, that sofa, was causing problems. It was too long and a smidgen too wide and as a consequence could not be manoeuvred into the ground. A professor of mechanical engineering from the Indian Institute of Technology had been summoned. He, in turn, had summoned a civil engineering colleague. Neither looked happy to be at Kotla at that hour. They hadn't yet formulated a solution to the problem.

Involved discussion was under way, however, and the authorities expressed optimism that the match would start as scheduled with all the VVVIPs in attendance and on the sofa.

Time, then, for a leisurely bath and breakfast. Mary came by to take my temperature and giggled when I asked her if I was hot.

The news post breakfast was even more promising. Shah, awake now, had realized that he had a PR nightmare on his hands. There was no insult intended, he was saying. As for the breach of protocol, surely he couldn't let his good friend, Keshavji, wait in the rain because his car was AWOL. The blame for that lay with the Indians – it wasn't his fault that the Indian driver was not there when needed. He had come with his hand extended in friendship; surely, the Indians would not misunderstand.

The PMO and External Affairs were still unavailable for comment. The Old Man was probably still asleep: there was no war on after all.

The talk shows were having a fine time. Opinion, hitherto solidly anti-Shah, was turning undecided after his press conference. Why, agitated Indians were asking, was the PM's car not there? Who was to blame? The bureaucracy, naturally. As they were for everything that was wrong with the country.

I felt a little uneasy at the turn opinion was taking. You couldn't blame the IAS for a cock-up concocted by Kapoor and his IFS cohorts. The record needed to be put straight and I decided to call in and clarify matters.

'What?' exclaimed the sweet young thing who answered the phone.

'Yes, there have been wholesale changes in the PMO. The IFS has taken charge of this visit and are responsible for this deplorable state of affairs.'

'Just a minute, sir.'

A few minutes and a more senior-sounding voice came on the line. A very well-known voice, as a matter of fact, and I knew I was on air.

'Yes, sir. What is your name, please?'

I thought swiftly. 'Purushottaman from Tirunelveli, sir,' I replied in my best Tamilian accent.

'Yes. Mr... er... er...'

'Think of it as Puru Shot a Man. Then it is simpler.'

'Ah, yes. Do you mind if I refer to you as Mr Man?'

'Yes, sir. No, sir. I mean to say I don't mind, sir.'

'What do you have to add to this controversy, Mr Man?'

'It is unfair to blame the entire bureaucracy for this, sir. One particular section of officers, namely the Indian Foreign Service, has recently taken control of several key posts in the Prime Minister's Office. In particular, a gentleman named Vikram

Kapoor, who has just moved from a posting in Africa. My information is that he and the driver of the PM's car were eating jalebis when they should have been fetching the car. Therefore, he is responsible for this terrible eventuality.'

I wasn't sure how Purushottamans from Tirunelveli actually spoke, but hoped that I was managing a passable imitation.

'This is a new angle entirely. May I ask you, sir, if this is just an unsubstantiated rumour or if there is a basis to your assertion?'

'I assure you that my assertion has every basis, sir. The cook at the banquet is my cousin brother on my mother's side and he assures me that he saw the two eating jalebis. Many jalebis, in fact. It is, therefore, a fact that the foreign service is to blame.'

'Thank you, Mr Man. You've added a new twist to this controversy. If anyone at the PMO is watching this programme, perhaps they might comment on this.'

I had learned from hard experience that half truths, once floated, gained currency and were difficult to deny. I had no doubt that Kapoor was responsible for the faux pas. He may or may not have been gorging himself on jalebis in the company of the driver, but that was beside the point. It was a nice story and denying it would make him look a bigger fool than he was.

I switched channels.

Kumudbenji, like any good politician, knew which way the wind was blowing. The anti-Shah rhetoric had been toned down and, even as I watched, one of her aides came over to whisper in her ear.

What I heard next was music to my ears.

'I have just received information,' she shrieked, 'that an officer from the foreign service is responsible for this mess.'

There was more, of course, but I could rest content in the knowledge that Kapoor had Kumudben to deal with on top of everything else.

15

Chaos

1

The start of the test match was nigh and I made myself comfortable. It had taken a while, but I was now able to appreciate the situation in which I found myself. Full salary plus benefits, meals from the Taj, a comfortable air-conditioned room, no work to do and all the time in the world to take in the test match.

Not bad at all.

I switched channels.

There was trouble at Kotla. The civil engineering professor had suggested demolishing a part of the stadium to let the sofa in. This had not gone down too well with the stadium authorities and he had stormed off in a huff. The mechanical engineering professor was hard at work on a Computer Aided Design program to try and figure out a way to manoeuvre in the sofa. The computer had knotted itself into an infinite loop and was refusing to respond to the good professor. He sat there, in full view of the TV cameras, looking as though he wished he was someplace else.

One of the commentators thought this was all very funny; most of the rest failed to appreciate the humour in the situation.

In the meanwhile, the start of the match had been postponed. Knots of officials stood and argued. Off to one side, I could see Kapoor shouting and gesticulating with the rest. The two teams practised desultorily and the crowd grew restive. The VVVIPs were still at their respective residences, waiting for the word to move. The minutes ticked by.

One of the commentators had a bright idea: a phone-in competition for suggestions on how to get a move on.

Get rid of the politicians, said one. Let them watch the match on television, said another. Why can't they sit on plastic chairs like everyone else? asked a third. All well and nice, but what was needed was a constructive suggestion. I called in, as Purushottaman.

'Why don't they saw the sofa into shorter lengths?' I asked. 'Then they can use Araldite or something similar to glue the pieces back together.'

An hour or so later, the reconstituted sofa was in place. I have to say that it made for a grand sight – impressive, resplendent even, as it sat on the grass in the pale, watery sunshine. I had created a problem for myself, though: I had won a refrigerator along with tickets for the match as a reward for my efforts. The refrigerator would be presented along with the Man of the Match awards. Problem was that as a public servant, I was expected to maintain the highest standards of probity and accepting rewards was just not on. I have always prided myself on my ethics and was not about to be tripped up by some two-bit phone-in contest. The easiest thing would have been to give them a false telephone number along with the false name. This I had neglected to do and was dreading the prospect of telephone calls asking for Purushottaman.

2

The delay had caused other problems. The roads to Kotla had been sanitized in accordance with security procedures. The procedures called for traffic to be held up for a maximum of twenty minutes. An hour-and-a-half had now gone by. The traffic cops had not been told of the delays and had not let any traffic through. The result: gridlock throughout New Delhi – the paralysis had spread as far as Azadpur in the north and the Rajasthan border in the south. Uttar Pradesh was effectively cut off as was Haryana. Connaught Place, sorry, Rajiv Gandhi Chowk, was a giant parking lot as were the sidewalks and any other bit of available space. Frantic calls by delayed office-goers on their mobiles had jammed the airwaves. Frantic attempts at freeing up some bandwidth had caused further communications breakdowns and all air traffic was being diverted away from Delhi. I heaved a sigh of relief; the dreaded telephone call was unlikely to come any time soon.

I had further cause for satisfaction as well: Vikram Kapoor was making a royal mess of things. I sat back, sipped a glass of nimbu pani and gratefully surveyed the situation.

Things got worse.

A lot stranded near Parliament got restive and started shouting slogans against politicians, who, they assumed, were responsible for this and various other grievances. Their proposition found many takers. A helicopter-based TV crew got good shots of a mob storming Parliament. The gridlock meant that no reinforcements were forthcoming, so the security staff quickly locked themselves into the Central Hall of Parliament.

One could see that the mob was enjoying this unfettered access to the realm of the rulers.

3

At some point, a decision was made to bring the VVVIPs to the match by helicopter. The sanitized route was desanitized and the gridlocked traffic filled it instantly, causing another gridlock. It was a good thing Shah was in Delhi – this would have been an ideal opportunity for a Pakistani attack.

There were any number of heartrending tales filling the airwaves – people stranded en route to airports and stations, people unable to make it to hospitals, children lost in the general confusion, and so on. Unfortunate, certainly, but also increasingly monotonous. I switched back to cricket.

The helicopters (separate ones for Shah and the Old Man, I was glad to see. Kapoor had learned one lesson at least) had landed. The overnight rains meant that dust was not kicked up and I could see the haggard look on Kapoor's face as he helped the Old Man down the steps. The Old Man looked grim and barely acknowledged Kapoor. I couldn't help but be pleased. My known experience in handling crises had been overlooked not once, but twice, in favour of Dixit's and Kapoor's slick and superficial ways and I was entitled to a modicum of personal satisfaction even if there had been a serious breach of national security.

Shah looked preoccupied as well. He must have been following developments on TV and was perhaps rueing the missed opportunities. Either that or he was worried about what the generals would say about the limousine caper. Another missed opportunity: he could have kidnapped the Old Man and there was nothing we could have done short of war if he had decided to drive on to Wagah.

In any event, joy at the prospect of the test match was absent.

An MI 24 brought in the first lot of ministers, but the two PMs did not wait for them. The players' introductions were brief and grim and the two made for the sofa. I had made charts detailing where the ministers were to sit and I was glad to see that Kapoor had the good sense to use these. But wait – something odd was going on. Naturally enough, the cameras were trained on the two PMs, so at first, they did not pick up what was going on offstage.

One of the ministers had jumped the gun and seated himself next to the Old Man. Kapoor had been busy assigning ministers to seats and, along with the real assignee, was startled to find this prime spot occupied. The man seated there, a tobacco magnate from Warangal, refused to move. The real assignee, Hukum Singh Rathore from Jaipur, refused to accept anything less. Hot words were exchanged. Kapoor attempted some diplomatic mediation. It was soon clear that he had never attempted mediation between politicians. Dealing with Somali warlords was one thing; dealing with ministers from the GNC was something else again. The Old Man refused to intervene – it was evident from his expression that the matter was beneath him. Shah looked on eagerly: Indian democracy clearly had features of interest.

Kapoor pleaded and cajoled – in vain. Hukum Singh Rathore was a Rajput and Rajputs did not take things like this lying down. Or standing up, as was the case here. He slapped Subbarama Reddy from Warangal who, in his dealings with the Naxalites in his district, had learnt a thing or two about firmness. He pulled out a revolver.

I should point out that ever since jumbo cabinets had become the order of the day, I had insisted on ministers being frisked before being allowed near the Old Man to prevent just this sort of eventuality. Indian democracy, in the course of its meanderings, had bred many deviants and one could never be too sure. Kapoor had not learnt his lesson – too many years attending posh cocktail parties had dulled what edge he had.

But even he must have realized what two stray shots could do to Indo-Pak relations. He flung himself on Reddy with admirable alacrity and the gun fell down. Some SPG types materialized. One went for the gun and the others were soon wrestling with the ministers. Rathore, spying a vacant spot on the sofa, made for it, dragging three SPG jawans along with him. They fell with a thud onto the sofa. The sofa began to sink into the ground, which was sodden from the overnight rain. It tilted over. Shah got up as did the handful of pre-geriatric ministers. The geriatrics, the Old Man included, keeled over helplessly with the sofa.

16

Wee Willie Winkie

1

The telephone rang. I let it ring. The last thing I
wanted was the call for Purushottaman. Besides,
events on TV were far too interesting. It stopped,
then started again. I glared at it in annoyance.
Why couldn't one of the nurses outside answer it?
It continued to ring, defying my attempts to will it
to stop. Finally Mary came in.

'Why aren't you answering the phone?' she
wanted to know.

I glared at her coldly.

'Joint secretaries to the Government of India do
not answer telephones.'

'You are a very funny man,' she giggled.

I let that pass. She picked up the phone and
after a couple of 'yes-es' passed it on to me. 'Prime
Minister wants to speak to you,' she giggled.

'Why don't you answer the phone, Swami?' he
asked querulously.

'I was busy, sir.'

'Still having bathroom problems?'

'Of course not, sir.'

'Never mind. I won't tell anyone. Now this Kapoor has made a big mess.'

'I know, sir.'

'How do you know?'

'I have been watching things on TV, sir.'

'You mean... you mean... you mean...'

You see, when one of the SPG chaps had finally lifted the Old Man off the sofa, a bit of his dhoti had got stuck and stayed behind. The nation had been treated to, shall we say, a free show.

'Unfortunately, yes, sir.'

'And what are you doing sitting in that bloody hospital? Get here at once.'

'Sir?'

'What?'

'What about Kapoor, sir?'

'Send him back wherever he was.'

'Wherever?'

'Yes, you heard me. Wherever. Now get here immediately.'

'Yes, sir,' I said happily.

2

The man was eighty-two, he had spent six decades and more in the service of the nation and one would have thought that he deserved a modicum of respect. But no.

Wee Willie Winkie
By Our Correspondent

New Delhi: The nation was treated to a rare sight as the first test match between India and Pakistan got under way here after a series of snafus that delayed the start of the match and left the city in the grip of chaos. The player introductions done with, the two Prime Ministers had barely settled into the huge custom-built sofa that took up one end of the ground when it began sinking into the turf. Overnight rain doubtless played a part in this. The presence of a large number of freeloading ministers (the sofa had evidently been designed to accommodate as many of these luminaries as possible) tipped the balance, so to speak, and their insistent presence hampered efforts to rescue those unable to get up.

The over-seventy crowd, which made up the majority, found themselves flailing and screaming as the ground threatened to swallow them up. The crowd, restive thanks to the delayed start, finally found something to laugh about. Members of the Special Protection Group had to swing into action, bodily lifting the ministers and carrying them to safety. The crowd soon had even more

to laugh about. The Prime Minister's
dhoti refused to part from its moorings
on the sofa and stayed behind as he
was lifted up. The crowd (and, via
TV, a large international audience)
were treated to the spectacle of the
prime-ministerial willie. It was a wee
willie as willies go and exposure to
the crisp morning air certainly did
not permit any excesses. Many moments
passed before the prime- ministerial
dignity was restored. The laughter by
now was contagious. Some two dozen
spectators were admitted to the Maulana
Azad Hospital for seizures caused by
uncontrollable laughter.
Several political commentators were
of the opinion that the exposure of
the crown jewels as fake would limit
Mr Motwani's ability to control his
unwieldy coalition....

There was more such drivel, but I shall not bore you
with it. The other newspapers were not far behind
in their cavalier treatment of a sensitive matter. The
TV channels were no better. The offending moments
were shown and reshown.

I wondered what women thought of it all. Indian
women are modest by nature and apt to take offence
at this sort of thing. Did anyone spare a moment
to consider their feelings? No.

I have felt all along that the press has had far too
free a run. The days of the Emergency (1975–77)

stand out as beacons in an otherwise dull and dismal landscape. They were days when there was a sense of national purpose and when the news reported was news worth reporting. I sketched out a series of amendments to the respective Acts, which would restore matters to a more desirable state.

2

The Old Man was still shaken when I took my proposals to him that evening.

'Swami, I shall have to resign,' he said. He looked at me dully, he lay draped like an old sack on the sofa – even the Choli Girl had failed to work her usual magic. It was a worn and defeated Old Man that I found myself looking at. I felt tears starting in my eyes as the poignancy of the scene sank in.

'No, sir, you shouldn't resign.'

I have to say that I didn't find myself too convincing.

'The nation needs you, sir, in this hour of need,' I continued. 'A crisis has always brought out the best in you. You must stay and fight on.'

'The Opposition is tabling a no-confidence motion in Parliament.'

'That is no reason to resign, sir. You have a large and growing majority. Anyway, what is this no-confidence motion all about?'

'All that gaddar yesterday. They are accusing me of mismanaging the country.'

'That was just a traffic jam, sir.'

'Arre, but I have to go there and answer them.'

'I shall stay up all night and write up position papers to guide your answers, sir. The Opposition will not know what hit them. In any case, it was not your fault. Blame that Kapoor. He is the cause of all your problems. And if they are seeking your resignation about a traffic jam, all Opposition- led states, starting with Bihar, will have to resign. We can offer to have a Joint Parliamentary Committee to prepare a White Paper on the subject. They will need to study traffic systems in other countries as well before reaching a conclusion...'

'Swami, you are babbling.'

'I'm only trying to help you, sir.' I have to say that I was hurt at this cavalier dismissal of my efforts.

'Swami, you are wasting my time. I expected better of you.'

'I don't understand, sir.'

'Arre, I know that you don't understand. You are obviously not understanding. I want to watch the test match tomorrow, not listen to those idiots in Parliament.'

'Oh.'

'If I resign, I can watch the match. Now do you understand?'

'Yes, sir. But you don't have to resign for that, sir.'

'Then tell me how I can watch the match.'

'I'll find a way, sir.'

'Good.'

3

The leader of the Opposition, Bhanwarlal Kesarilal Tiwari (BKT), was not what you would expect in a mature and functioning democracy. Blame the Opposition for that. They were a fractious lot and what leaders they had could agree on only one thing – that none of the others should be the leader of the Opposition. This meant that the chosen one was no leader and no threat.

The problem was that BKT was a self-righteous and uptight so-and-so. For instance, he kept a herd of cows in his official residence and milked them himself at four each morning. The cows proved none too enthusiastic about their wake-up call and their early morning protests upset the neighbours. Also upsetting was his habit of collecting the manure and plastering manure cakes on the wall to dry. Fine in Gaya or Ayodhya, but not in Lutyens' Delhi. Then there was his Gandhian insistence on abstinence from vices real or imagined, which meant that invitations to get-togethers hosted by him were received with dread.

This moral rectitude meant that the normal give-and-take which formed the bedrock of parliamentary democracy was not possible. Ultimately, the Old Man had no choice but to encourage mass defections in order to ensure continuing governance.

The Old Man has been lampooned and pilloried in the media for his role in the formation of the GNC and the jumbo cabinet. The blame for all this lay elsewhere and I'm happy to be able to put the record straight.

When I went to see BKT, it was past ten, but he was still up and about. He had just delivered a calf and was busy sweeping his veranda. He was not pleased to see me.

'You?'

'Yes, sir,' I replied.

'What do you want?'

'We need to talk, sir.'

'I have to spin thread on my charkha after this.'

'We can talk while you spin, sir.'

He glared at me. 'You youngsters, you are the reason why this country is going to the dogs.'

I was past forty, my relatives insisted that I was too old for marriage, and here he was, clubbing me with the nation's youth.

'Why dogs, sir? Dogs are wonderful creatures. Ask Maneka Gandhi.'

'How can you talk and spin at the same time? You need to pay attention to what you are doing. It is a lesson I learned from Gandhiji. What does Maneka Gandhi know about all this?'

'I don't know, sir. I'll ask her the next time we meet.'

'You wait until I finish spinning.'

'How long will that be, sir?'

'One hour. But since you are waiting, I can reduce it by ten minutes.'

'Thank you, sir.'

He set up his charkha and the ball of cotton. No sofas for BKT. I sat alongside on the floor and watched.

'I usually have a glass of cow's urine while I spin,' he said. 'Would you like some?'

'No thanks, sir. Could I have a Pepsi instead?'

'Cow's urine is good for your health. It is all in the *Yajur Veda*. The first urine of the morning is especially good. I collect it and keep it in the fridge. The ancients used clay pots. I did, too, but the neighbours kept complaining. One of their dogs tried to drink some from the pot, but it fell inside and drowned. Was that my fault? No. But quarrelling with the neighbours is not good either. That is in the *Artha Shastra*. So, now, I keep it in the refrigerator. I will get you also a glass.'

I sat and watched him spin. There was something rural about the whole scene, including the smell from my untouched glass.

'What you were saying about dogs,' he said suddenly, interrupting his spinning.

'What did I say?'

'You see, dogs are not Indian.'

'Why?'

'There is no mention of dogs in the Vedas. That means there were no dogs here in the Vedic age. Cows are Indian though.'

'Oh.'

'Yes, that is why people talk about the Cow Belt. There is no Dog Belt, you see.'

I felt like telling him that it was probably because belts were made of cows rather than dogs, but let it pass. He went back to his spinning.

I was nodding off when he suddenly announced that he was done. He went inside to put away his charkha and spun thread and I took the opportunity to empty the glass into the nearest flower pot.

'Ah, you've finished your drink?' he asked, spotting the empty glass. 'How did you like it?'

'Not as good as Pepsi, sir.'

'You mix it with some soda and it is even better than this Pepsi thing. You get dyspepsia drinking this Pepsi thing. I serve urine with soda at all my get-togethers. They all think it is whisky and drink it – improves their health.'

I had been aware of a sour smell emanating from the garden and now I knew what it was. Clearly, no one had been taken in. And no wonder the neighbours were so upset.

'What do you want, young man?' he asked, settling down to business.

'This no-confidence motion, sir.'

'What about it?'

'You know it is going to fail, sir. You don't have the numbers.'

'Yes. Motwani makes everyone a minister. What do I have to offer?'

'Cow's urine, sir?'

'Yes, there is that, but I don't limit it to those in my party. A healthy politician makes for a healthy country. They all know that I am generous to them even after they have defected and become ministers. How many ministers are there now?'

'One hundred and seventy-six, sir.'

'Nehru had nine in his first cabinet.'

'Yes, sir. But to get back to the no-confidence motion, why go through with it when you know you are going to lose?'

'It is my duty.'

'Duty?'

'Yes, to bring to everyone's attention how this country is being mismanaged.'

'Mismanaged?'

'Did you see what happened this morning?'

'Yes, sir.'

'One of my cows wandered out and was hit by a scooterist on the pavement. Why was he on the pavement? Because of the traffic jam. Why was there a traffic jam? Because of your Mr Motwani's mismanagement. Because of this traffic jam, I couldn't even take the cow to the hospital.'

'You should have called the PMO, sir. We would have sent a helicopter to airlift your cow.'

'I tried calling, but all the phone lines were busy – too busy with this cricket match, you people. While my poor cow suffered.'

'I'll make sure I send a veterinary surgeon immediately, sir. There is no need for the no-confidence motion.'

'You can send your surgeon, but I stand by my motion. The nation needs to be aware of this misgovernance.'

'The nation is busy with the test match. Your motion will have greater visibility if you postpone it until after the match.'

'What match? Why should I postpone my motion for a mere match?'

'Sir, you are letting your ego get the better of you. That is not a good thing. It says so in the *Rig Veda*.'

'That is the *Bhagvad Gita*, not the *Rig Veda* – not always a reliable source of advice. The ancients followed the Vedas, not the Gita. I follow the ancients.'

We debated theology and a host of other matters over the next two hours, but the man proved stubborn. There was no way I could induce him to postpone his motion. He was definitely not anal retentive when it came to his motion. A little anal retention, I wanted to tell the Old Man who had castigated me for it, was sometimes a desirable quality.

4

It was three in the morning. My shoulders bowed in defeat, I sat in my office, thinking of ways to empty a pot of cow's urine (fresh and steaming) on BKT's thick skull when something occurred to me. I picked up the phone.

The commissioner of police was groggy with sleep. He had had a long day as well and I felt bad waking him up for what was at best a long shot. Still, the Old Man wanted to watch the match and I hadn't much time.

'A scooterist who ran into a cow?'

'Yes, on Janpath.'

'Swami, most scooterists who run into cows don't complain to the police.'

'This was on a sidewalk. It was BKT's cow.'

'Not one of those cows.'

'Unfortunately, yes.'

'Swami, I'm sick and tired of BKT's cows. They can go to hell. If he wants to complain about a scooterist running into one of his cows, he can go to hell. What the hell was his cow doing on the sidewalk anyway? Why didn't he keep his bloody gate shut?'

'Commissioner sahib, I too don't give two hoots about BKT's cows. I don't even care if the bloody cow dies. I want the scooterist, so I can get him to file a case against BKT for letting his cow loose on the sidewalk. I'm sure there is some law against it – wanton cruelty to animals or something.'

'Oh. So you want a case against BKT? Hmm. I'll see what I can do. But what if the scooterist has not filed a police complaint?'

'Check all the scooter dealerships to see if a scooter was brought in for repair or something.'

'Hmm. Big job, but I'll put a thousand constables on it.'

'Vital national interests are at stake, commissioner sahib.'

'I don't doubt it since you are calling at this hour. BKT needs to be fixed. He even tried to serve me urine and soda at a reception.'

'He is getting cheap in his old age. He's cut out the soda now.'

'God! I'll get to work, Swami. Will keep you posted.'

5

Sanjeev Sachdeva looked scared as he was ushered into my office. I suppose anyone would be if he had been dragged out of his house by the cops and taken in a high speed motorcade to the PMO without a word of explanation. I tried to put him at ease. 'A cup of coffee, Mr Sachdeva?'

He stared at me with hunted eyes and was unable to get a word out.

'There is nothing to be concerned about, Mr Sachdeva. I'm having a cup of coffee. Won't you join me?'

More of the rabbit-caught-in-the-headlights look. The sod needed gentle handling. I made a mental note to constitute a committee of secretaries to look into the police–citizenry interface with a view to introducing a more human and less inhuman touch. But that was in the future. I needed to deal with Sachdeva now.

The coffee was served.

'Did you know, Mr Sachdeva, that coffee originated in the Ethiopian highlands and that the drink was first savoured in the Arabian Peninsula, possibly in the regions adjoining the Horn of Africa? Strange to say, the Yemenis might well have been the first coffee drinkers.'

I took a sip. 'This particular blend is a mixture of Brazilian and Colombian Arabica. The very name, Arabica, suggests a geographic origin for these beans. This blend is specially prepared for the PMO by Fortnum's of London. You are therefore in a position of privilege, Mr Sachdeva.'

I took another sip. Sachdeva's coffee sat untouched.

'Is anything the matter Mr Sachdeva?'

'Aap Hindi bolte hai?'

So that was it. I switched to Hindi. 'Is anything the matter?'

'I swear to you, I did nothing wrong. There was a big traffic jam. I was getting late for work. Everyone was climbing on the sidewalk. I was not the first one. How did I know that cow was going to be there? I am very fond of cows, I tell you. I worship them. I hit it only by mistake. I tried to swerve, but the cow was still in the way. I tried to brake, but you know how these brakes are. Also, there was a bus behind me and I was afraid that if I braked too hard, it would hit me. I cannot afford another scooter, sir. I am just a poor salesman.'

'I know you have done no wrong.'

'Then you won't send me to jail, sir? My aged mother lives with me. I am the only son. She has a weak heart and...'

'Listen, Sachdeva. You are not going to jail. Nothing is going to happen to you.'

'Can I call up my mother and tell her?'

'Here, call up.'

I tried not to overhear the emotional conversation that followed.

'Okay,' he said, once the tears had dried and his emotions were finally under control. 'What do you want?'

'I want you to file a complaint with the police.'

'Complaint? Police? Sir, I don't want to have anything to do with the police.'

'Nothing will happen to you. The police are expecting you.'

'But what do I complain about, sir?'

'The cow.'

'I told you, sir, I didn't mean to hit the cow.'

'Arre baba! Can't you understand? Nobody is blaming you. That bloody cow had no business being there.'

Some dim measure of understanding began to seep in. 'Yes, sir. It is very difficult, sir. Lots of stray cattle on the roads. That and these Red Line buses. Very difficult for us scooter riders.'

'Exactly. So, if that cow belonged to someone, he is to blame for your accident.'

'But how do I know whose cow it is?'

'You don't worry about that. Just tell the police where the cow was and what time you hit it. They will investigate.'

'Which police station should I file my complaint in? I've never filed a police complaint in my life.'

'You don't worry about all that. I'll send you in my car.'

So, that was one problem solved. The commissioner's dragnet had worked, even if it meant half the police force staying up all night. Now they would act on the complaint and summon BKT. They would keep him away from Parliament all day, which meant that the no-confidence motion could not go ahead. The Old Man could watch his match in peace without needing to resort to a resignation drama.

17

Cricket Capers

1

It wasn't as though nothing else had happened on that eventful day.

Cricketers are a fastidious lot and some of the measures taken to ensure the comfort of the VVVIPs caused play to be held up. For instance, they needed to be protected from the sun and a number of umbrellas had been provided for the purpose. Kapoor had chosen some bright colours, far too bright for my taste, but then subtlety had never been the IFS' strong point. Anyway, the Pakistanis, who were batting, objected to the distracting array of umbrellas and play was held up while replacements were sought.

Have you ever seen a white umbrella on sale in India? I thought not. The resources of the Central government, the Delhi state government and the BCCI were all brought to bear on the problem, to no avail. Finally, I suggested just painting the umbrellas white and this worked, save for three ministers fainting from the paint fumes. This wasn't all bad as three alternate ministers could be accommodated on the sofa.

Being an important occasion and aware that they were on TV, the ministers were all in starched white khadi. This was a relief as getting them to change would have been awkward. Shah, though, was in a green safari suit and seated where the batsmen were unlikely to miss his presence. Luckily, the Pakistanis were batting and could not bring themselves to complain to their PM about his dress. The match went on, but the Indians were unable to capitalize on this advantage. They clearly lacked our Mussoorie training and looked unfocused and disoriented as they went about their business. Leading them was Snehasish Mukherjee, who took the field late as he had nicked himself shaving and dropped three catches while on the field. Ready as always to assign blame elsewhere, he cited the wooden platform as having distracted his players.

2

Wooden platform? Well, after the sofa had been pulled out, it couldn't very well be put back where it had been. There was no alternative location either – the rain had been democratic in its favours. Tense moments passed as the crowd yelled its disapproval

and the SPG herded the VVVIPs into the Ladies'
Room for their safety (the Gents was deemed
vulnerable to terrorist strikes). I hit on the idea of
a large wooden platform and this was put in place.
This was fine with the Old Man, Shah, the security
lot and by me. Not so Mr Mukherjee. Perhaps his
shaving incident had thrown him off kilter, but
he was adamant that the platform would not do.
Too distracting for the fielders, was his verdict. A
resounding set of boos was the crowd's response.
Finally, we painted the bloody platform green and
he dropped his three catches.

Given the restiveness of the crowd, we didn't wait
for the paint to dry, and as a result, the VVVIPs all
had green and rather sticky soles by the end of the
day. Shah alone was pleased. He made sure the Old
Man and the ministers all knew that his suit and
their soles matched and that they both resembled
Pakistan's national colour. The Old Man did not
take this ribbing too well.

By the end of the day, his face resembled India's
national colour.

3

He had more to say when we got home.

The platform, first of all.

'Swami, Shah is making fun of me.'

'What is he saying, sir?'

'Have you seen my chappals?'

'Which chappals, sir?'

The Old Man was partial to chappals. He had an informal deal with Bata, wherein he got a pair of each new model they released. There were seven hundred odd pairs when I last counted. (Counting the Old Man's chappals is the first task assigned to any official joining the PMO. The Old Man is rather possessive about his chappals and doesn't like any filched. A Directorate of Chappals had been set up to deal with this, but BKT got wind of it and it was disbanded in a hurry before he went public with the news. Hence, the counting.)

'The ones I wore to the match.' Flesh coloured plastic ones, quite unworthy of prime-ministerial feet.

'Yes, sir.' I refrained from further comment. There was a yawning gap in our tastes. I preferred Gucci loafers.

'Well, they got this green paint on them and Shah kept saying they were Islamic chappals. I tell you, I don't like it. He is my guest, so I can't have him thrown out. You have to do something about it. I don't want to spend the next four days listening to Shah making fun of me.'

'Maybe the paint will dry overnight, sir.'

'I don't care. Change the colour.'

'But the Indian captain insisted that it be painted green. He said it would affect the fielders.'

'Who is this captain?'

'Snehasish Mukherjee, sir.'

'How many catches did he drop?'

'Three, sir.'

'One right in front of us. Shah laughed. Like a bloody hyena. He made fun of me. Change this Mukherjee. Change the colour also.'

The colour was unsatisfactory and, Mukherjee or no Mukherjee, it had to be changed.

The Old Man was not done. 'Swami, that platform is no good.'

A day's worth of ministerial comings and goings meant that it had gradually sunk into the ground and, at the close of play, was barely visible above the grass. Something had to be done.

'I know sir.'

'I don't like these wooden platforms.'

'It wasn't that bad, sir.'

It was my idea. It was something I had thought of in a moment of crisis when no one else had anything useful to say, and I didn't really care for people being wise after the event.

'Yes, yes, but a concrete platform will be better.'

'Concrete, sir? Concrete takes time to set.'

'I don't know about all that. I want a concrete platform tomorrow.'

'Did Shah make fun of the platform as well?'

He glared at me. 'Who told you?'

'Just a wild guess, sir.'

'I don't like your wild guesses, Swami. I also don't like Shah telling me what is wrong with my country. Who does he think he is? Prime minister of Europe?'

'Europe does not have a prime minister, sir.'

'Who told you? Still guessing wildly, eh? Swami, you are pushing your luck. Now go and get that concrete platform made.'

It was sometime then that he got news of BKT's deviousness. It was a busy night, but I got a concrete platform set in place in addition to dealing with the BKT problem.

4

Having dealt with Sachdeva, I needed to consider the problem of the platform's colour. A neutral shade with a sponsor's logo would have been ideal, but I knew that the Old Man would not be satisfied. He needed something with which to needle Shah. I finally hit on the idea of naming the platform Ram Janmabhoomi and painting the whole thing saffron. Garish, yes, but it would go well with the Old Man's chappals.

Ram Janmabhoomi had to be inaugurated and the Old Man agreed to this with alacrity. As I had anticipated, he was much taken with my colour scheme. He loved cutting ribbons and I had arranged for a saffron one for him to cut. There was a minor hitch that I hadn't anticipated. Post-inauguration, Ram Janmabhoomi became sacred ground. Well, not quite, but the Old Man took off his sandals before setting foot on it. The others had no choice but to follow, Shah doing so most reluctantly. I could see that he had generals on his mind. The others, though, had paint on their feet. Plus, the concrete was cold. Ministerial displeasure came through loud and clear.

The VVVIPs were bundled off to the Ladies' Room once more as I implored Sri Parthasarathy Swami for inspiration. He must have been heartily sick of me, but a sleepless night had left me bereft of ideas and I could only hope that as an Iyengar, I had a special dispensation with Him.

I did.

It took a while to get the coir carpet from IGI and I had time both to repaint the platform (the ministers had left their footprints all over it) and to reflect on the irony of a commie carpet being used to cover non-secular ground. Teach those godless bastards a thing or two.

During all this, Mukherjee hung around with a scowl on his face. It got to the point where I couldn't take it any more.

'What's the matter, Mukherjee? Cut yourself shaving again?'

'Shut up, you bloody bastard.'

'Do you have any idea who you are talking to?'

'Who are you to talk to me like that?'

'You dropped three catches. As a patriotic Indian, I have every right to talk to you like that.'

'This bloody platform and these bloody ministers distracted me. Now they have gone and painted it red.'

'Saffron.'

'Saffron, red, they are all the bloody same.'

'No, they are not. Saffron is an Indian colour mentioned in the Vedas. Red is a foreign colour mentioned in the writings of Chairman Mao.'

'You can't sight the ball against this. As a cricketer, it is all the same, saffron or red.'

'Yesterday, it was green and you still dropped three catches.'

'Somebody started clapping before I caught the ball.'

'You mean they clapped before you dropped the ball.'

'Who the hell are you and who allowed you here anyway?'

'I should tell you that the PM wants you dropped from the team.'

'What can that old fart do?'

Mukherjee was making my blood boil. 'The PM has invited the BCCI chief for lunch. I am in charge of drawing up the agenda for the lunch.'

He backed down. 'Anyone can drop catches,' he said defensively. 'I nicked myself shaving. It hurt. It still hurts.'

'Change your razor then,' I said curtly before walking away. One can spend only so much time arguing with a skunk.

Mukherjee dropped four more catches that day before stubbing his toe on the platform. I had a word with the Old Man and, shortly after, Mukherjee was carted off the field and it was announced that he would take no further part in the series. As a politician of the old school, he had no patience with people who confused saffron with red.

18

Saffron Matters

1

Seven dropped catches, a nick and a stubbed toe later, Pakistan was in a commanding position. The Indians were in disarray. Shah had forgotten that he was on Ram Janmabhoomi and was cackling with glee.

The Old Man sat in grumpy silence. At one point, he whispered to me that listening to BKT in Parliament was preferable to this. This was saying a lot. He loved his cricket. He had even, he told me, led a band of rustic villagers to victory against the Brits in the days before Independence. This was shortly after he had seen *Lagaan* and perhaps his memory had played one trick too many on him (he once confided in me that he was envious of Aamir Khan for getting Aishwarya Rai in the Coke ad), but it showed his love of the game.

It was a lovely day for cricket with blue skies and a fresh looking outfield, but none of this made an impression on him. Mohanty's cultural shows did nothing to cheer him up either, possibly because Shah showed an unseemly interest in some of the female dancers (the Old Man knew that a man of his age was not expected to show a public interest in these matters and felt this was not fair). Mukherjee had spoilt the day for him.

2

There was something else as well, something we were unaware of just then as we watched disaster after disaster hit India on the field – something brewing in a major centre of Hinduism in the Himalayan foothills.

As a layman with a passing interest in religion and rituals, my assumption was that the average monk passed his day in meditation, study and prayer. Throw in a discourse or two, a debate perhaps on some point that had remained obscure through the centuries, a few hurried moments spent on meals and there would appear to be no time left for worldly distractions.

My assumptions were rudely shattered. The first intimation of trouble came in a phone call from a friendly journalist. I had to strain hard to hear him on my mobile over the disapproving roars from the crowd.

'Swami, someone is accusing the government of religious blasphemy.'

'What?'

'Yes. Some chap, wait a minute, name of Mahant Niroopananda Saraswati, have you heard of him?'

'Sounds vaguely familiar.'

'Got an ashram in Kasauni.'

'Oh. Kasauni. Yes.'

'Anyway, he is upset that the government has started building the Ram Janmabhoomi temple in Delhi.'

'What?'

'He has quoted extensively from the scriptures to prove that Lord Ram's birthplace is in Ayodhya.'

'He doesn't have to tell me that. I've read the Ramayana. Written by C. Rajagopalachari, an Iyengar like me.'

'What? Valmiki wrote it. That is what we were taught in school. Have they changed the textbooks since?'

'Rajagopalachari wrote the modern English version. Valmiki didn't know English. I don't know Sanskrit. Hence, Rajagopalachari.'

'Oh.'

'Anyway, what is this mahant threatening to do?'

'I saw a bit of it on TV. He is planning a march to Delhi or some such. He is talking about throwing out this blaspheming government – couldn't catch it all. The mahant was talking in Sanskrit and the chap translating it was into Sanskritized Hindi, which I cannot follow too well. Get hold of a TV. See for yourself.'

Easier said than done. There were a number of TVs, but all were tuned in to the match. It looked as though the replays were more popular than the match itself. I couldn't find a discreet way to switch to a news channel without arousing suspicions.

After much searching, I found a TV in the Ladies' Room.

3

The restroom had been done up in a great hurry to accommodate the VVVIPs and now boasted a fresh coat of paint and air-conditioning, in addition to the TV set. I switched to the news and settled down to watch.

The mahant was media savvy all right. He was seated outdoors and had the snow-clad Himalayas as a backdrop. He had a trishul in one hand and a spear in the other. He was draped in saffron and had ashes of different hues smeared across his forehead. Around him stood his acolytes, some with spears and others with what looked suspiciously like AK-47s.

None looked pleased.

'The government has reneged on its promise,' he was saying. 'Instead of building a temple in Ayodhya, they are cheating us by building one in Delhi.'

This was rank nonsense. I called up NDTV to issue an official denial. Was I sure that no temple was being constructed in Delhi?

'Listen,' I said, 'I cannot vouch for any private construction. But the government was not involved in the construction of any temple, for Lord Ram or anyone else.'

I was about to add that the government was not in the business of building temples when there was a piercing scream some six inches behind me. I fell off the chair, dropping my mobile as I did so.

It was an incredibly fat lady trying to pull on her salwar. Acres of fat stood in the way. I stared at her, stunned and nonplussed. She continued to scream. It took me a moment or two to realize that I was in the Ladies' Room and that she was objecting to my presence there. I hastened to clarify things.

'I'm sorry, madam. I just came to watch TV. I was told that some important news was coming through that I needed to watch.'

She took a deep breath and continued to scream.

'Madam,' I said desperately. 'I am not a peeping Tom. I'll turn my back to you. I don't want to stare at you. I am a high government official. This is a matter of utmost importance, I assure you. Please stop screaming.'

Through all this, she kept up her screaming. I remembered Sachdeva and switched to Hindi. 'Madam, please. I am not what you think I am.'

I could hear answering shouts outside and footsteps coming closer. I turned to touch her feet. 'Please, I beg your forgiveness.'

She tried to kick me and I hung on for dear life. The cops burst in. Fatso burst into tears. I had my arms around her thighs to prevent further bodily damage.

I was, I have to admit, in a compromising position.

4

'I tell you I am from the PMO. I am on an important assignment.'

A short spell in a cell in Daryaganj Jail, and now interrogation. I was standing, my hands and feet were shackled and my blazer and pants had been replaced by some dirty striped garb.

There was no sign of my Gucci loafers.

'You were in the ladies' bathroom,' said the head cop implacably.

'Yes, I know that. I only wanted to find a TV that was not showing the match. There was some important news I needed to watch.'

'You are not a lady,' he continued as if I hadn't spoken.

'I know that. You didn't have to pull my undies off to establish that. I have a moustache, for heaven's sake.'

'Then you tried to molest a lady.'

'No, I did not. This is all a terrible misunderstanding. Where is my mobile? I want to make a call. I can prove I am not what you think I am.'

'Statement made by Constable Lilavati states that you were hugging Mrs Dhillon and had one hand on her buttocks.'

'I was trying to protect myself. She was kicking me. If my hand was on her buttocks, it was by accident.'

'Prisoner admits he handled her buttocks,' he said to a sidekick, who wrote it down.

'I did not!' I screamed. 'I admit to no such thing. If I touched her, it was in self-defence.'

'Prisoner admits Mrs Dhillon kicked him in self-defence,' he said to the sidekick.

'Goddammit! I want to speak to a lawyer!'

'Statement made by Constable Mangal Ram confirms statement made by Constable Lilavati. Suspect had one hand on Mrs Dhillon's left buttock.'

'Dammit! I wouldn't want to finger her butt even if I had a chance.'

He looked at me curiously. 'Why?'

'Because she is fat and ugly, that's why.'

He shook his head. 'Mrs Dhillon is a beautiful lady. Embodiment of Punjabi beauty. First you finger her, then you insult her.'

This was all too much. I waved my arms in distress, forgetting that they had been shackled. I lost my balance and fell over. The cops laughed.

I cried.

5

'Swami, you were in the Ladies' Room, I am told.' The Old Man was on the line.

'It was all a big misunderstanding, sir.'

'You are really having problems with your number two, then.'

'No, sir. It was not that at all.'

'I thought the doctors had cured your problem. It must be very difficult if it keeps coming suddenly like that.'

'It doesn't come suddenly like that, sir.'

'To go to the Ladies' Room. Must have been coming very quickly. I tell you what, you get these adult diapers. Big ones for grown-ups like us. I will have AIIMS send you a supply.'

'Sir, please, sir.'

'Later, you can go see a foreign specialist. Obviously, these AIIMS doctors have not been able to cure you. By the way, Shah also sends his best wishes.'

'You mean you told Shah?'

'Arre, with the match going the way it is, anything to keep him from talking about cricket. He said his father has the same problem. He has nurses to wash his bum though.'

'Sir, there is a serious problem that we need to discuss.'

'We are discussing your serious problem.'

'I don't have a problem. That is not what I had in mind. There is this mahant in Kasauni...'

'Yes, yes. Now I remember. I need you here, Swami. Serious problem. I am getting you released. Come here immediately.'

It turned out that tiring of Shah's leg pulling, the Old Man had looked around for me and, seeing that I was missing, sent for me. It took a while, but eventually, the connection between the missing personal secretary and Mrs Dhillon's alleged assailant was made. The Daryaganj head cop's face was a study when he realized just whom he had slammed in jail.

As for Mrs Dhillon, it was soon established that Mr Dhillon's residence in New Friends Colony had been built without permission. A retraction of her allegations was soon obtained. There was nothing to compensate me, though, for my trauma.

Mrs Dhillon's thighs were the stuff of recurring nightmares.

My other problem, which I realized when I exited Daryaganj Police Station in the full glare of TV cameras, was that the Old Man had gone to town with the news of my alleged incontinence. Having one's bowel movements discussed in public was something I could have done without. Ditto the many expressions and looks of sympathy I received.

Neeta's was typical. 'Swami, I had no idea...'

'I'm perfectly all right.'

'I know it is something you don't really want to talk about.'

'I said that I'm perfectly all right.'

'I sensed things were not fully okay with you.'

'How many times do I have to say that I'm perfectly all right?'

'My thoughts are with you, Swami. Have you tried eating bananas?'

6

I was glad to be able to grapple with the mahant problem instead. Events had spiralled out of control thanks to Mrs Dhillon and the cops. BKT's cow had kept him busy till evening, but he was now out and ready to embrace the mahant's cause.

'I am against globalization, multinationals and pseudo-secularism,' he said, reading from a paper. His pronunciation was atrocious and it was clear he didn't really understand what he was saying. But then few politicians do.

'This government,' he continued, 'seeks to destroy Indian culture and mislead the youth. What sort of a country do we have where a man is not free to allow his cows to graze where they please? What sort of country do we have where a cricket match takes precedence over a parliamentary discussion on misgovernance?' He stumbled over 'precedence', 'parliamentary' and 'misgovernance' and barely made it past 'discussion'. He needed a good speechwriter, one who could adapt a speech to his abilities. Else he should have stuck to Hindi and taken a chance on BBC's translators.

'What sort of a country do we have where Lord Ram's birthplace is arbitrarily shifted from Ayodhya to Delhi, where non-secular Pakistanis can stamp on it? I am upset at this debasement of our values and shall commence a fast until death under Mahatma Gandhi's statue in Parliament.'

No one took BKT too seriously and there were no follow-up questions. If he was disappointed, he didn't show it. I suppose he was used to being ignored.

The mahant meanwhile was making for Delhi in a cavalcade of vehicles painted saffron for the occasion. He carried with him a few clods of earth supposedly from Ayodhya and allegedly from Lord Ram's birthplace. He stopped at various villages and towns on the way to allow the masses to ogle the clods and pray to them. The clods soon generated a devoted following. By the time I caught up with him, the cavalcade was miles long with bullock carts and stragglers on foot bringing up the rear. The BBC and CNN were taking an undue interest in this bit of modern Indian culture. The newsreaders could barely contain their smirks.

India was being ridiculed by the world press and all I could do was watch.

19

A Kashmiri Problem

1

In the next room, the Old Man and Shah were watching as well. My absence from the former's side at the match meant that he was free to put his hoof in it. This he had done, by inviting Shah for a private showing of you-know-what. And now the two were watching the Choli Girl in the next room.

I could hear loud cackles and the occasional loud expression of pleasure. Being a true Punjab da puttar, Shah was effusive in his outpourings. I could hear him loud and clear and so could, in all likelihood, the entire neighbourhood. This bonhomie was good as far as it went: good atmospherics made for good politics and the odd breakthrough in diplomacy, as such, was no bad thing. What I was concerned about was the possibility of Shah initiating a strategic leak to the press. After all, he had a history of rushing to the press with half-baked truths. And a nasty habit of scoring cheap points, instead of engaging in substantive diplomacy. The fact is that I wouldn't have put it past him to spend the evening enjoying the Old Man's hospitality as well as the Choli Girl's sexy moves and then go running off to the press with the scoop on what a dirty man the Old Man really was. The generals and mullahs would doubtless have something to say about decadent Hinduism and the need for a more virulent strain of Islam.

I began to wish I was back at AIIMS with Miss Mary and her giggles for company. The hoots of appreciative laughter from the next room meant that I couldn't think straight. There is only so much an expert juggler can handle and I had my hands – and thoughts – full with the mahant, the Old Man, Shah and the Choli Girl. Not to mention Miss Mary, whose giggles echoed noisily through my thoughts.

2

There was much backslapping as the two emerged from the late night show. The Old Man looked years younger and Shah could barely contain his snorting.

'We have made a bet,' the Old Man announced.

'Sir?'

'We have decided that we have spent enough years fighting and arguing about Kashmir.'

I wasn't sure I wanted to hear the rest. 'Yes, sir?'

'Go on, you tell him,' he continued, nudging Shah.

'No, no. The pleasure is yours entirely. Besides you are the host of the evening. I am only your guest.'

'Okay, I'll tell him. We have solved the Kashmir problem.'

'Solved?'

'Arre, can't you hear? Solved – once and for all.'

'How, sir?'

'If they win the match, we keep Kashmir, and if we win the match, we give them Kashmir.'

The blood drained from my face and my feet wobbled. I had to grab a chair to keep from falling. 'Sir, you can't do this, sir.'

'Why not? I am the Prime Minister of India.'

'You have to take Parliament... the country... into confidence. There are likely to be serious geopolitical ramifications...'

'Arre, woh sab baad mein karenge. This is a gentleman's agreement.'

'Yes,' piped up Shah. 'Let the match get over, then we can discuss the modalities of implementation and all such.'

'But...'

'No buts. We have decided.'

'But what if it is a tie?'

'Tie?' exclaimed the betting duo in unison.

'Yes. What if the match ends in a tie?'

'We hadn't thought of that,' said Shah thoughtfully.

'Arre, we will just toss a coin,' said the Old Man. The sporting spirit had him in its grip.

'That is too chancy.' Shah looked worried.

'What are you looking so worried about?' inquired the Old Man expansively. 'Cricket is a game of glorious uncertainties. Just like coin tossing. After all, a game of cricket starts with the toss of a coin. How nice it would be if it ended with the toss of a coin!'

'But cricket is also a game of skill. May the best team win and all that.'

'Arre, why don't you like my tossing a coin idea? I thought it was a very good idea. What do you suggest, Swami?'

Damn! I didn't like being put on the spot like this. Decisions needed to be considered ones with all aspects of the situation duly weighed and taken into account. Now, with Kashmir in the balance, I was being hurried into a rash and ill-considered decision. I could well foresee my being called to account if things went wrong. The betting duo was looking at me expectantly.

I did the best I could under the circumstances.

'If it is a tie, we keep Kashmir,' I said finally.

The Old Man looked pleased, Shah looked thoughtful. 'Okay,' he said. 'Deal?'

They shook hands on it.

3

'What have you done, sir?'

Shah had left and I was alone with the Old Man.

'Arre, haven't you seen the score?'

I had. It didn't look good for us.

'Swami, we are going to lose the match. There is no way we can win the match. So, we lose the match and get to keep Kashmir. The nation will be so proud of me. What a fitting climax to my career!'

'Sir...'

'And your suggestion about the tie – that was brilliant. I shall remember it. Perhaps I shall even mention it in my autobiography. I am always willing to give credit for a good idea. That was a good idea.'

'You are planning to write your autobiography sir?'

'Arre, someone will write it for me. But it will be my autobiography.'

'But sir...'

'Why this but-but-butting? You are always but-but-butting.'

'Not always, sir.'

'Now you are splitting hairs.'

'Sir, this bet...'

'First but, then bet – what is the matter? You have to admit that I got a good deal.'

'Sir, you are betting on the Pakistani team winning.'

'Look at the score, you silly idiot!'

'I am not an idiot, sir, I am an IAS officer. And may I remind you of how they lost to Bangladesh in that World Cup match? How they lost to Australia? How they lost to England in the test series? They lost to England, sir, and if they lost to England, they can lose to anyone. They are past masters at this.'

'But we have that Mukherjee. How can they lose if we have Mukherjee in our team? I have thought of all of this already. Eighty-two years old and still with a sharp mind. How many catches has he dropped?'

'Seven so far, sir, but...'

'Again but-but-butting.'

'Mukherjee is in hospital with a stubbed toe. As per your request, he is taking no further part in the series, sir. Without him, we might pull it off. Laxman is in our team, sir.'

'Ram, Laxman, I don't want to hear of all this. You take care of this Ram–Laxman business. Get Mukherjee out of hospital, do what you need to do, just make sure we lose. I am going to sleep.'

'Could you give me written orders, sir?'

'I will give you written orders sending you to Mogadishu. Now get to work.'

4

'Swami?'

'Yes?'

'Shah speaking.'

'Is anything the matter, sir?' It was one in the morning.

'No, no. Nothing urgent. I wanted to have a discussion with you.' He was speaking in a low voice. There was something conspiratorial about his tone. I had had a long and tiresome day and was not in a mood to procure girls or whatever it was he wanted.

'And what do you wish to discuss at' – I glanced at my watch – 'one-oh-seven in the morning, sir?' Withering sarcasm, or so I thought.

'One-oh-nine, according to my watch. But that doesn't matter. I want to talk about the software business.'

'Software business? Now?'

'Don't raise your voice.'

'I'm not raising my voice. I'm only exclaiming.'

'Then don't exclaim. You see, it is like this. I want Pakistan to march into the future.'

'Yes, sir.'

'And software is the future.'

'Along with biotechnology and nanotechnology, sir.'

'What?'

'Our government had McKinsey and Co. look into the future and they informed us that software, biotechnology and nanotechnology were like a three-legged stool for the future.'

'I prefer four legged sofas myself, but I want to discuss software, not furniture. You see, I am very impressed by the products of your software industry.'

'Yes?'

'And also how well they cooperate with the government.'

'Yes?'

'I would like a special project done. Discreetly, of course.'

'Most, if not all, software company heads would be asleep now, sir. But I can arrange for a meeting, perhaps after the match is over.'

'I don't want a meeting. I want you to take care of it for me.'

This was getting stranger and stranger. 'But sir...'

'You also, Swami? I thought only our bureaucrats did this but-but-butting business.'

'No, sir, but...'

'Again.'

'Sir, I cannot be involved in decisions or negotiations involving the Government of Pakistan.'

'Who said this is for the Government of Pakistan? The generals take care of all that. This is for me.'

'For you?'

'Yes, for me personally.'

'Do you need some pirated software?'

'That I can get in China. Good friends of ours, the Chinese.'

'We know that. What do you need, sir?'

'This is a matter of discretion. That is why I am speaking only to you.'

'Yes, sir. What is it?'

'You know that movie Keshavji showed me?'

'That one?'

'Yes, with special effects and all.'

'Do you want a copy of it?'

'No. Not exactly. I want *Lagaan*.'

'Oh.'

'With special effects and all.'

'What special effects, sir?'

'You know what they did to the Choli Girl?'

'Oh, that. You want it done to the *Lagaan* heroine?'

'No, no. My wife will not like that. She gets jealous sometimes. I want done to the hero.'

'To the hero?'

'Don't misunderstand me. I studied in England, but I'm not like that. It is for my father – to take his mind off the nurses.'

20

Nuanced Negotiations

1

News that the mahant was headed for Delhi with the clods of earth from Ayodhya had spread. As dawn broke, the great unwashed masses poured into Delhi by train, bus, lorry, bullock cart and anything else they could think of. One naked sadhu was seated on his pet tiger and appeared to be high on pot.

'Could you explain what you are doing, sir?' the lady from BBC wanted to know.

He took a couple of deep puffs and mumbled something.

'This sadhu,' said the lady, turning to the camera, 'is seeking moksha, the Hindu version of salvation.'

'How do you plan to seek salvation, sir?'

Another mumble or two.

'He wishes to prostrate himself at the birthplace of Lord Ram.'

'Do you find riding this tiger comfortable?'

Mumble, mumble.

'He sold his elephant to a circus and now has to make do with this tiger.'

I could see the joker from CNN awaiting his turn. There were no terrorist attacks, earthquakes, typhoons, fires, no speeches by the US President, no genocides in Africa or the Balkans, nothing in Kashmir, even Fidel Castro's pipe hadn't cracked or exploded. Nothing. Nothing at all to distract the world press from one naked crackpot smoking dope and making his way into Delhi on his tiger.

The mahant, having started this nonsense, was nowhere in evidence. This was worrying. The cavalcade could not be stopped until I stopped the mahant. The mahant could not be stopped until he was found.

2

I tried BKT. He was off milking his cows and wasn't too pleased when I called.

'What is it?' he asked churlishly.

'It is about the mahant, sir,' I said. I needed to tread very cautiously. He didn't know that I was behind the Sachdeva business, but was probably still sore that his no-confidence motion had become a victim of political gridlock.

'I thought you wanted to talk about my fast.'

'Your fast?'

'Didn't you see the news yesterday? I held a press conference. It was carried by BBC and CNN, but nothing at all in Doordarshan. You are muzzling my voice. Why should I talk to you?'

'I'm sorry, sir, but there was no disrespect intended.'

'Half an hour of news and not one mention of my fast until death. And then you say there is no disrespect? You are a very cheeky man.'

'There were technical problems, sir. You see, the concerned minister was at the match and wasn't available to vet the news. So they ran the previous day's news. I'll make sure you are on Doordarshan tonight.'

'These cricket matches, they are no good. People waste their time watching cricket. Your minister also wastes his time and misses my fast.'

'I'll make sure you are the lead news tonight, sir.'

'I am starting my fast at ten. You must ensure that the Doordarshan fellows are there.'

'I'll make a note of it, sir. Where do you plan to start your fast?'

'Under Gandhiji's statue in Parliament.'

'Would you require a shamiana?'

'Of course. Also durries. And pillows and cushions. No need for fans, though. It is quite cool.'

'Mineral water, sir?'

'I am on a fast until death.'

'Gandhiji always sipped water when he was fasting until death.'

'Are you sure?'

'Yes, sir. Otherwise, he might have died of thirst. You are planning to die of hunger, not thirst, aren't you, sir?'

'Actually, between you and me, I'm not planning to die.'

'Oh.'

'You can be of some use to me, actually.'

'I'll be happy to help, sir.'

'You see, people don't respect honest politicians like me any more.'

'You are very well respected, sir.'

'No, I'm not. Did you see my press conference? Oh, you just told me you didn't. Technical problems at Doordarshan.'

'Yes, sir.'

'If you had seen it... how shall I say this... there were no questions.'

'No questions?'

'Yes. I read out my statement and there were no questions. Not even one. If I had been a respected politician, at least one question would have been there.'

'That was very inconsiderate, sir. I'll instruct Doordarshan to ask you some questions when you commence your fast.'

'Much appreciated. But I need more help.'

'Yes, sir?'

'I need someone to appeal to me to call off the fast.'

'Ah. I'll see what I can do.'

'I'll tell you what I really want.'

'Yes?'

'Could you get the PM to appeal to me?'

'He has a busy day ahead of him, but I'll appeal to him to appeal to you. If he doesn't agree, would it be okay if the Rashtrapatiji appeals instead?'

'Well... okay... but I would really prefer the PM.'

'I'll see what I can do. You see, he was a bit annoyed when you tabled that no-confidence motion.'

'Tell him I didn't really mean it. If I hadn't done it, my MPs would have been angry with me. What was I supposed to do? Tell him I'm sorry.'

'When do you want the appeal, sir? Tomorrow?'

'No, no, no, no, no. I am an old man. I can't go a full day and night without food. Five o'clock this evening will be all right.'

'Do you want me to arrange for a glass of nimbu pani to call off the fast?'

'Yes, please. Your cooperation is much appreciated.'

'Would you need some supporters to sit with you while you fast?'

'Yes, yes. Thank you.'

I suddenly remembered the reason for my call. I had been meaning to discuss the mahant when the SOB cleverly sidetracked me. One needed to be wary when dealing with these old urine-swilling politicians. They were experts at getting what they wanted while conceding little.

'There is only one problem, sir.'

'Problem? What problem? I thought we had settled everything?'

'You would want maximum publicity for your fast, wouldn't you sir?'

'Of course. And you promised that Doordarshan...'

'That I'll take care of. But the other networks... BBC, CNN, CNBC, they might not have crews available to cover your fast.'

'But why? When the leader of the Opposition goes on a fast until death, it is big news, is it not?'

'It is, sir. And as I said, there is no problem as far as Doordarshan is concerned. They will be seized of the importance of the occasion. But these foreign networks, they are more intransigent.'

'In... what?'

'What I mean to say is that they are all caught up with the mahant and his march to Delhi. They think that is big news.'

'How can they? Here I am planning a fast until death and...'

'I agree that you are more important. Even the PM knows that you are more important. But these foreigners... what can I say, sir?'

'What do you suggest? I would like BBC and all to cover my fast. After all, grave national issues are concerned and the world needs to be told about it.'

'Yes, sir. If this mahant can be persuaded to call off his march, they might send their crews to cover your fast.'

'Good suggestion. You get him to call off his march.'

'I can't. First of all, I don't know where he is. Second, he is opposed to the policies of this government. He will not listen to me even if I find out where he is. If you want BBC coverage, you must find him, sir, and persuade him to call off his march.'

'He is very upset about this Ram Janmabhoomi business. How could you claim that Lord Ram was born in Delhi? He was born in Ayodhya, as we all know.'

'I know that. This was just meant to be a symbolic janmabhoomi, not the real thing.'

'But the mahant does not believe that.'

'Tell him that we've changed the name.'

'What do you plan to call it?'

'The Babri Masjid.'

'Good.'

'So you'll take care of the mahant?'

'I'll do that. And you make sure my fast is well covered on TV.'

3

Dealing with politicians is easy – they speak a language that is clear and unambiguous. They are businesslike, and once the nub of the problem is identified, negotiations are reasonably straightforward. Not so cricketers. They are childish and petulant, they have huge egos, and they are incapable of rational social intercourse. Having a stubbed toe makes matters worse.

I could hear Mukherjee a long way off as I made my way down the long hospital corridor to his room. He was complaining insistently about something, and as I drew closer, I made out what it was. Someone had served him dust tea, instead of the Lapsang Souchong to which he was accustomed and this had upset him. Making matters worse was the fact that no one knew what Lapsang Souchong was.

Mukherjee: 'Doesn't anyone in this bloody place know what Lapsang Souchong is?'

Voice: 'Pardon sir, but the liquor shops don't open this early in the morning.'

M: 'What the fuck are you talking about?'

V: 'You wanted this drink. I assure you that I will ensure adequate supplies so you won't have this problem tomorrow.'

M: 'It is not that kind of drink, you blithering idiot!'

V: 'This shop, they carry all kinds of drink. Please, sir, you write on a paper, I will get it – whatever kind of drink it is.'

I stepped in at this point. 'Morning, Mukherjee! Missing your morning cuppa, eh?' I said with as much good cheer as I could muster. He was in a foul mood, my mission was a delicate one and the atmosphere was most definitely not conducive to a man-to-cricketer discussion.

'Who the fuck are you?'

'Swami...'

'Go fuck yourself, Swami.'

'There are technical difficulties in carrying out your instructions to the letter. But I might be able to obtain that Lapsang you were inquiring about.'

'You know what Lapsang Souchong is?'

'But, of course. I...'

'One joker here thought that Lapsang was the Dalai Lama's real name.'

'And this gentleman here thought that it was an alcoholic beverage. I overheard a bit of that conversation.'

'Who are you, anyway? Your face is vaguely familiar.'

'As I was about to add before you broke in, I am the PM's personal secretary. I happen to be a senior officer in the IAS.'

'You were that busybody at the ground. Now I remember.'

I let the slur pass.

'I was meaning to ask someone,' he continued, 'and I may as well ask you. Whose bloody idea was it to put that bloody platform right in the middle of the ground?'

It wasn't nice having one's brainwaves being rubbished by a mere cricketer. It wasn't the time to take issue with a bloody minded cricketer either, so I took refuge in a technicality.

'It wasn't in the middle of the ground. It was off to one side, if my memory serves me right.'

'That's beside the point. It was in my way. I stubbed my toe on it. Do you want to see my toe?'

I didn't, but had to take a peek, given my mission. I'll spare you the details. I'll say this, though – it reinforced my opinion that Mukherjee was one spoilt cry baby.

'What do you think?'

I fished around for the right words. 'Must have been painful.'

'Painful? I could barely stand. I now know what people feel like when they lose their limbs.'

'How do they feel?'

'Like how I felt when I stubbed my toe.'

'The PM sent me along to inquire about your toe.'

'Tell him I can barely stand. The next time you hold a press conference, you can tell the Press that I need to go to Australia for treatment.'

'Australia?'

'Yes, they have experts in sports medicine.'

'The PM was hoping that you would be in a position to lead our comeback.'

'I can barely stand. Our comeback will have to wait.'

'The PM was hoping you would play through your pain.'

'Fat chance! I have my future career to think of. I don't want to be on crutches for the rest of my life.'

'The PM has a big bet riding on this match.'

'Big deal. He can afford to lose a few bucks. Me, my career is at stake.'

'The bet is with the Pakistani PM. This is one bet he doesn't want to lose.'

'All he can think of is his bet. Doesn't he or anyone else care about my poor toe?'

'The collective prayers of the country are with your toe.'

'I should bloody well hope so. After all I have done for the country...'

'The PM feels that only you can turn this match around.'

'He was very curt when I introduced the players to him.'

'He was annoyed because of all the delays. He didn't even speak to his wife that morning.'

Technically correct, but I thought it wise not to tell him that he hadn't spoken to his wife in years, the said wife having attained moksha. I assumed that someone as self-absorbed as Mukherjee would be unaware of the good lady's demise.

'Oh? Is that so?'

'Indeed.'

'Then it was not meant against me personally?'

'Not at all. The PM is a great fan of yours. As indeed is the rest of the country.'

'What about you?'

'That goes without saying.'

'My toe... it could be permanently damaged...'

'Great victories are not achieved without sacrifices.'

'People tend to forget the sacrifices we cricketers make.'

'How can you be sure?' I paused for effect. 'The government can officially recognize your sacrifice,' I added meaningfully.

'What do you have in mind?'

'An Arjuna award.'

He looked unimpressed. 'The kabaddi coach in the chawl down the road got the Arjuna last year. Do you remember his name?'

'No.'

'Well?'

'A Padma Shri then.'

He hemmed and hawed.

'Listen, Gavaskar himself got only a Padma Bhushan. With all due respect to you, it would be difficult justifying anything other than a Padma Shri. Mind you, I think that you deserve much better, but there you are.'

'Okay,' he said finally. 'But are you sure you can pull it off?'

'I do have some influence,' I said with due modesty. 'And can exert it in favour of any candidate that I favour.'

'It is a weighty responsibility that you are thrusting on me, but for the sake of the country and since the PM himself has appealed to me, I shall endeavour to do my best.'

I thought it best not to tell him that the nominations for the Padma Shri came from the states and that the Centre had little say in the matter. We had a match to lose and I hadn't much time to do anything about it. I hadn't actually lied to him, after all, and if he needed educating on the ways of the national awards, there were plenty of others to do the job.

21

The Test

1

Mukherjee's appearance was greeted with a chorus of hoots and boos. The Old Man was in the process of nodding off and woke up with a start. When he saw what the noise was all about, he grinned broadly and couldn't resist throwing a few choice abuses Mukherjee's way.

I hurried to his side. 'I know how you feel, sir, but I told him you were a fan of his. He might get upset if he sees you.'

'Let him get upset. What is he going to do?'

'He might score a few runs, sir.'

'Oh, oh. I'll clap instead. By the way, what have you promised him?'

'A Padma Shri, sir.'

'But the states nominate the Padma Shris.'

'I know that, sir.'

He smiled once more. 'You are very clever, Swami, very clever indeed.'

High praise, but he was not telling me anything I didn't already know.

The Old Man's good humour was not reciprocated by Shah. He must have given his bet some thought and the sight of Mukherjee making his way ponderously to the wicket was not one that would have given him joy. He looked worried. Soon, he had even more reason to be worried as Mukherjee delivered a one-two punch that would have done Mike Tyson proud.

First up was a classic cock-up that resulted in Laxman getting run out. Mukherjee was a specialist in this sort of thing, but this one was memorable even by his standards. Laxman trudged back to the pavilion as Mukherjee stood around, looking hurt at the crowd's reaction. Storm clouds hovered over Shah's visage.

Next came a yorker aimed at Mukherjee's toe. Yes, that toe. Padma Shri or no Padma Shri, his instinct for self-preservation took over. The toe, his bat and the rest of his body got out of the way of the yorker with as much dignity as they could muster. The ball, finding nothing to halt or deflect its progress, duly knocked Mukherjee's leg stump out of the ground.

Mukherjee made his way back. A lesser man would have blanched at the reception he got. Mukherjee took it in his stride. He had seen and heard it all before.

Shah couldn't possibly take this double whammy in his stride. He had summoned an aide and was whispering urgently. If he had a set of worry beads, he would have fingered them furiously. He didn't, so he fidgeted, cracked his knuckles and generally looked very upset. I thought for a moment of the matches Pakistan had lost – the one against Bangladesh, for instance. But then I looked up at the scoreboard. There was no way we could lose. After all, you can drag a horse to a stream, but you cannot make it drink. They could do all they wanted, but couldn't make our lads score the winning runs.

2

Meanwhile, BKT was proving an unexpected hit. Mohanty's crew was holding the fort during the drinks break and, along with the rest of the crowd, I too had decided to take a break. I had popped over to see what the networks were up to. (Not the Ladies' Room this time. I had no desire (no pun intended) for a replay of the Mrs Dhillon episode and had had the BCCI set up a media room for my use.) There he was under the shamiana, lounging on his mattress, a scattering of sidekicks coming and going. The joker with the tiger had also showed up and had taken up residence under the shamiana. This was not what had caught the BBC's eye, however.

Arranged in a row in front of BKT were a number of bottles filled with a golden liquid. He was holding forth on the many virtues of the bottles' contents. The BBC was lapping it all up. CNN and the rest were awaiting their turn impatiently. India was once more proving an unending source of exotica.

3

Over in the Indian dressing room, a drama of a different sort was taking place. Mukherjee's stoicism in the face of the baying crowd was worth an honourable mention or at least a footnote in the general scheme of things. I have to say that the sight of him walking back after his double fiasco moved me. I had roused him from his comfortable hospital bed and knowingly egged him on to his humiliation. He had taken it like a man.

Now, safe within the confines of the dressing room and well out of sight or hearing of the baying mob, he was bawling like a child. Reason: his exertions had aggravated the toe. His teammates were having none of it – they were pointedly seated as far from him as they could be and were giving their undivided attention to the goings on in the field.

The team physio had apparently told him that there was nothing wrong with him that a cube of ice couldn't cure. This had upset Mukherjee. He had arthoscopic surgery, preferably in Australia, in mind.

I tried to soothe him. 'You must be upset,' I said.

'You are bloody right I'm upset,' he bawled.

'It's all in the game. Win some, lose some.'

'Lose some? After all I've done, he tells me I don't need to go to Australia.'

'Never mind. There is always the second innings.'

'Second innings? What second innings?'

'We need you now more than ever. Who is going to score our winning runs?'

'You saw me. You saw how difficult it was for me to move. That idiot Laxman almost ran me out.'

That wasn't quite what I had seen, but I let it pass. 'For the sake of India, Mukherjee...'

'Did you hear those bastards boo me? They deserve a loss if you ask me.'

'I'm sure they didn't mean it personally.'

'I don't care. I've had enough of this. I've sacrificed enough for my country. I want my trip to Australia.'

'The PM says...'

'Fuck the PM.'

'In that case, I am constrained to state that my offer to favourably consider your case for a Padma Shri no longer stands.'

'Fuck the Padma Shri.'

My blood boiled. I picked up the ice cube and jammed it down on his toe.

4

'What is this, Swami?'

The Old Man and I had stopped by at Parliament to appeal to BKT to call off his fast. He was in his shamiana all right, but was sharing space and attention with a second shamiana that had come up next to him.

Occupying central stage under the second shamiana was Mukherjee. He too had begun a fast until death. When he saw me, he began screaming.

'That's the man! That's the man! He is the one who has damaged my foot irreparably. He hammered it with an ice pick! He's the man!'

'What is this, Swami?'

'Well, sir, what really happened was...'

'Why is he here? If he goes on hunger strike, we will win. I thought I told you to make sure he plays.'

'I did, sir. He played. You saw him play.'

I noticed BKT gesticulating frantically.

'One minute, sir, I'll be right back.' I walked over to BKT.

'What is he doing there? I'm hungry. I want that nimbu pani now. I had ordered some samosas and now they are getting cold.'

'He is coming, don't you worry. There is a microwave oven in the Parliament canteen and they can reheat the samosas for you. And they have some ice, too, if you want your nimbu pani cold.'

'Yes, get me some ice. But that fellow there,' he indicated Mukherjee who, even as we looked on, wiggled his toe around for the TV johnnies, 'he comes along and all the TV fellows have gone there. Now no one will witness the breaking of my fast.'

'Not to worry, Tiwariji, wherever the PM goes, the TV crews follow. They will follow him here.'

'He gets all the publicity and I get none.'

'But he is the PM.'

'And I am the leader of the Opposition. I am also a VVVIP.'

'I'll make sure I mention that in my daily press briefing.'

'Good. But... but... why is that fellow showing his feet like that? Why are they interested in his feet?'

'It is his toe, not his feet, that they are interested in and it is too long a story to go into here. Ask him yourself once you are done with your fast. I'll call the PM now.'

It was a ceremony with a hoary past, one that had, over the years, marked the ebb and flow of Indian politics and become as much a part of India as the Ganga and the Himalayas. It harkened back to the days of the Independence struggle, days when the likes of Gandhiji strode the landscape like colossuses. My eyes dimmed with tears as I watched the age old ritual re-enacted.

The Old Man was a pro in these matters. He knew the TV cameras were rolling and he showed genuine feeling as he whispered the requisite words into BKT's ear. BKT knew the drill as well: the reluctance to interrupt his journey to moksha and the reluctance to accept the proffered glass of nimbu pani made for moving theatre. In another age and in other circumstances, Shakespeare might have picked BKT to play Hamlet.

As it was, the polity had to make do with the assurance that the leader of the Opposition had agreed to continue to discharge his duties to them.

5

The TV crews had moved over to record this important episode in Indian history and I could see that Mukherjee wasn't pleased at the turn events had taken. I walked over to see if he would listen to reason.

'There is no need to resort to such drastic measures,' I began.

'What the hell is going on there?'

'Mr Bhanwarlal Kesarilal Tiwari is being prevailed upon to call off his fast.'

'Who the hell is he? I am fasting here and no one is paying any attention to me.'

'They might if you took the field tomorrow.'

'How the fuck do you expect me to take the field after what you did to my toe?'

'You said you wanted to go to Australia and I was merely trying to help you along.'

'Well, it didn't work. The physio said that an ice compress was all that I needed.'

'I thought as much. Mine was an ice compress of sorts, if you see what I mean.'

'I don't. It was more like an ice pick. Anyway, what is the PM doing now?'

'Giving Tiwariji a glass of nimbu pani.'

'Sweet or salted?'

'Sweet.'

'Can you ask him to give me a glass as well? I'm hungry.'

I stared at him coldly. 'The PM is a very busy man. He can't be bothered with handing out nimbu pani to every Indian who wants one. He believes in people helping themselves. His motto is: ask not what the PM can do for you, ask what you can do for the PM. And what you can do for the PM is to get out from this ridiculous shamiana and go join your team.'

'But I can't do that. I am on a fast until death and I cannot call it off just like that.'

'You are a cricketer, not a politician. Call it off. No one will notice.'

'That is what you think. People are concerned about me. Did you see the TV crews? They were all asking questions. Even Pepsi called. They are sending a rep across tomorrow.'

'To film you calling off your fast with a glass of Pepsi?'

'How did you know that? It was supposed to be a secret.'

'It will be too late anyway. Coca-Cola is filming Hrithik Roshan calling off his fast with a Coke even as we speak.'

'But that is not fair. It is not even their idea. They stole our idea. They always steal our ideas.'

'Have it out with Coke then. I'll leave you to it. All the best with Pepsi tomorrow. Ciao.'

'No! You can't leave me like this! I'm hungry. I'll be cold tonight.'

'You should have thought of all that earlier. Never act precipitately. That's my motto and you can borrow it for the night.'

'Wait! No! Wait! I'll do what the PM wants. I'll be on the field tomorrow.'

I had been walking away, but now I sauntered back. 'Did I hear what I thought I heard?'

'Yes! I'll do all for my country!'

'And Australia?'

'You heard the physio. All I need is an ice compress.'

'Pepsi?'

'Screw them. I don't like multinationals myself. A glass of nimbu pani will do fine. Sweet, if you don't mind. But please ask the PM to appeal to me. I mean... what will my girlfriend think if I call it off just like that?'

The Old Man was notably frosty as he went through the motions. He preferred the predictability of politics to the uncertainties of cricket. Mukherjee was no thespian. I finally had to write the words out for him and he was wooden in his delivery. It took three takes to get everything right.

The glass of nimbu pani was handed over. He took a gulp, made a face and almost spat it out on camera. I had spiked it with salt, you see. Troublesome cricketers deserve nothing less. Especially after all the increased blood pressure he had given me.

6

It was a day without precedent in the history of cricket. There were some who harked back to 1981, when Ian Botham turned certain defeat into victory. Others with longer memories and better cricket libraries talked of Gilbert Jessop and the innings he played in 1902, again turning certain defeat into victory.

Mukherjee and his boys parlayed certain victory into defeat. No, I take that back. They almost won, despite themselves, until I intervened to save the day for the Old Man. Mukherjee helped, of course. But then, I didn't expect any less from him.

A Topsy Turvy Day's Cricket
By Our Correspondent

New Delhi: Cricket at Kotla today was a riotous mix of the bizarre, the sublime and the ridiculous. The Indians lost, of course, but their path to

that inevitable outcome was marked by
twists and turns of a kind never seen
before on (or off) a cricket field.
The dramatis personae included a goat,
an IAS officer, a horde of angry ants
and a cricketer nursing an injured
toe. This correspondent has covered
cricket at the highest level for the
past twenty-three years and can claim
knowledge of matches going back a good
deal further in time. None, to his
knowledge, has come close to this one
for sheer unexpected drama.

So much so that a performance of
Manipuri Bhangra (something evidently
concocted by a Sardar settled in
Manipur) during the luncheon interval
seemed normal in comparison. This
despite the fact that the Sardar wore
a frock, while his accompanists had
to strive hard to keep their top hats
from blowing away.

The day began poorly for India. The
tail contrived to lose their wickets
in the face of some sloppy bowling by
the Pakistanis. A juicy half volley
was dragged back on to the stumps; a
run out where the batsmen chased each
other up and down the wicket as the
Pakistanis tossed the ball from end
to end (causing a colleague to remark
that both teams were trying to lose
the match); and, a fitting cap to the

innings, a batsman, his eye on one
of the more distant buildings, given
out for obstructing the fielder when he
barged into the wicketkeeper, who was
attempting to catch a throw. This last
decision was vociferously protested by
the Pakistanis. The crowd entered the
argument as well amidst scenes that
must have been painful to those who
think of cricket as a civilized game.
All this to little avail. The umpires,
having delivered their decision, walked
off leaving India staring at a huge
deficit. The last three wickets had
added only three runs and the deficit
was two hundred and thirty.

Pakistan's decision to not enforce the
follow-on would have come as a major
surprise in any match other than this
one. The goings-on in the field had
inured us to such surprises.

Even so, the Pakistan innings proved a
stunner. It lasted all of four overs
and totalled eight runs. This despite
a further six dropped catches by the
Indian captain, Snehasish Mukherjee,
bringing his match total to thirteen.
No records of dropped catches have
been kept, but it appears extremely
unlikely that Mukherjee's effort has
been bettered. All the Pakistan runs
were made as the batsmen crossed
over in anticipation of a Mukherjee

catch. The crowd was delirious at the turn of events. One dismissal in particular, where a misread run had both batsmen yelling at each other in the middle of the pitch, was the cause of much celebratory mirth. The sound of celebratory fireworks being set off elsewhere in the city could be heard as the wickets fell in rapid succession. The Pakistan total of eight marks a new low in the recorded history of test and first class cricket.

Unusually, the reactions of the two Prime Ministers did not echo the course the match was taking. Mr Shah looked ebullient and was seen in animated conversation even as his side threw away a huge advantage. Mr Motwani sat grimly through the proceedings and was seen shouting at his secretary at one point.

The target was an attainable one, given that the pitch was still true.

India's opening pair, Gupta and Sharma, took advantage of some very loose bowling to put on eighty runs in quick time. The crowd had regained its good humour and matters looked on course for a crowd pleasing ending. Laxman, coming in at the fall of Sharma's wicket, was soon in full flow. The hundred and fifty came up without any further loss. An Indian win appeared to be a mere formality when Gupta, attempting a hook, lost his balance and fell on his wicket. This brought in Mukherjee. Such was the crowd's good humour that only a scattering of boos greeted him.

Mukherjee later claimed that an irreparably injured toe had affected his game and that he had played only because of a direct appeal from the Prime Minister. This was denied later by an official from the PMO.

In any event, the hoots gained strength as he ran out first Laxman and then the next four who followed. In each case, the Pakistanis targeted Mukherjee, but he was too canny and cricket savvy to oblige. The hoots changed to cheers shortly thereafter. During a drinks break, Mukherjee sat down and evidently disturbed an ants' nest. The sight of him howling and jumping around in pain elicited the remark that this was the latest instalment of the cultural dances that have plagued the match. The resulting bites on Mukherjee's bottom meant that he could take no further part in the match...

7

I think I should take over at this point. The Press, in my experience, is an unreliable reporter of events.

Too often, they report things they don't see. In addition, they have a regrettable tendency to not report things they do see. As a result of this, the public has remained ignorant of the many initiatives taken on their behalf by the government, leading to their voicing completely unjustified complaints about bureaucrats, politicians and the government. The fact that the Press chooses to ignore the overall picture, the context as it were, when reporting the facts they choose to report only adds to the problem.

'Our Correspondent', whom I have quoted at length, was not immune to these tendencies. I am forced, therefore, to clarify matters by putting them in their proper context. I would like to add parenthetically that the term, 'our correspondent', involves a certain presumption on the part of the correspondent. He was not my correspondent, nor was he the correspondent of anyone else in my acquaintance. Technically, he should have referred to himself as 'a correspondent'. But that is a minor matter that I shall let pass.

Mukherjee's absence from the field meant that the team could regroup and rededicate itself to the pursuit of victory. This they did with a minimum of fuss. There were singles to be had and they took them. The Pakistanis were bowling gentle half volleys, which were treated with all the deference that a lobbed grenade or a North Korean made Hatf missile would command.

Each single brought victory closer. Each single took Kashmir further out of our grasp. Each single added to the Old Man's agony. I was sure he was planning to blame me for all this. I was not being paranoid. The look he shot me after every ball was one I had seen before – the look of a politician about to unload his crock of shit onto a bureaucrat.

I squirmed and looked away. Matters on the field were out of my hands. I had warned him about the Pakistanis and their cunning and nefarious ways. I had given him a blow by blow account of their previous match-throwing exploits. I had done all a bureaucrat could to steer him away from disaster. Instead, he had done a Yudhishthira.

Shah looked positively gleeful. He was indeed Duryodhana in all but name – and about to yank the sari off us by taking Kashmir away. There was little left to do but pray.

I prayed hard.

8

You may remember that Sikander was to be handed over ceremonially at the conclusion of the match. The match was scheduled to go on for five days. I had planned for at least four days of cricket and had not given much thought to Sikander.

Now, with singles coming off nearly every ball, the end of the match was nigh. I put in an SOS for Sikander, stressing the urgency of the situation.

The driver of the van bearing Sikander took me at my word, reaching Kotla in less time than I thought possible. Sikander, bumped and buffeted around by the careening van, was in a foul mood when he got to Kotla. It took six NSG commandos to subdue him and tie him to a post near the VVVIP sofa. There, he took out his frustration by attempting to break free. A section of the crowd that threw bottles and rubbish at him did not help matters.

Sikander was one angry goat and getting madder all the time.

9

Miracles do occur and sometimes two of them occur in quick succession. Sometimes they happen after I have prayed to Sri Parthasarathy Swami. As happened now. Against all odds and against the run of play, two wickets fell. Shah looked aghast. A smirk of sorts returned to the Old Man's face. The crock of shit was held in abeyance. Our hold on Kashmir strengthened, if only slightly. We were down to our last pair, but neither had shown any aptitude with the bat in the past.

The next few overs were a sheer farce. The Pakistanis tried all their tricks – full tosses, half volleys, balls bowled to one side with the entire field on the other. You name it, they tried it. Only to run up against the insurmountable obstacle of our incompetence. These two couldn't have batted to save their mothers. They swiped, they swatted, but they got nowhere close to the ball. The crowd watched with grim and growing frustration.

The tension mounted. I could hear my heart thumping away. Judging from the looks on their faces, so could the rest of the crowd. A hushed silence enveloped the proceedings. I prayed some more.

Suddenly, abruptly, the tension broke.

First, Sikander broke free. He had been chewing on his rope and managed to eat his way through. He now set off on a mad gallop around the ground.

At about the same time, number eleven made contact with the ball. It sailed skyward in a lazy arc. The batsmen started running. The Pakistanis gathered in a spot as far from the ball's path as they could. Sikander, on his second trip around the ground, caught sight of the ball and ran towards it. He made a perfect catch and continued on his manic run. The batsmen continued to run; the scoreboard continued to tick over.

The crowd was on their feet by now, cheering and shouting. The noise spurred Sikander on; he stepped on his accelerator and ran ever faster. The batsmen continued to run.

Disaster loomed. If this continued, they would score all the runs they needed. No one else was going to do anything to stop either Sikander or the batsmen. It had all come down to me. I flung myself at Sikander as he rushed past – no luck. He was way too quick for me. Flinging off my blazer (a Gucci blazer – I might as well remind the country of the sacrifices I have made for it), I ran after Sikander, shouting at him as I did so.

The batsmen continued to run, shrugging off my presence on the field.

Something – my voice, some intimation that he was being chased, something at any rate – got to Sikander. He stopped, turned and saw me. Perhaps he remembered me from the airport, perhaps it was the noise from the crowd. Whatever it was, he pawed the ground a few times before bending his head low and charging me.

I had never been charged by a goat before. A bull, yes, but never a goat. Another time, another place, I might have considered taking out my handkerchief (Hermes) and displaying my abilities as a matador (a skill they taught us in Mussoorie along with horse riding and other useful things). Not now.

I kept my eye on the ball even as he gave me the charge. Stepping aside at the very last minute, I wrapped my arms around him and, in one swift movement, extracted the ball from his mouth before tossing it to one of the Pakistanis who was standing nearby, gaping. Without thinking, he caught it. The bowler, stunned at the turn of events, made some sound, which the umpire took for an appeal. 'Out Caught' was his verdict. (And rightly so, I might add. The laws of cricket state that the ball must be caught on the full, that is, before touching the ground. Thanks to Sikander and my quick thinking, the ball never touched the ground before the Pakistani fielder caught it.)

We had lost the match.

And I, Swamy, joint secretary in the PMO, had snatched Kashmir from the jaws of a Baltistani goat.

22

Aftermath

Even the mightiest of steel girders can be weakened by time, stress and the weight of circumstances. I was a mere human – IAS, yes, but human for all of that – trying to serve his country to the best of his abilities. I, too, was laid low – by self-serving politics. I had expected a reaction – which Indian wants to lose to Pakistan? – but the volume and virulence of the vituperation stunned me.

I was hustled by the Old Man's NSG detail into the ladies' toilet – yes, that ladies' toilet – to protect me from a crowd that had developed temporary amnesia about Mukherjee. I could sense that the NSG's efforts on my behalf were half-hearted. Concern about the plight of a fellow human being was absent in the looks they gave me. I averted my eyes.

True to form, the Old Man didn't stand up for me. Instead, he pulled off the oldest trick from the politicians' handbook. He sent me to hospital.

The ambulance drivers' union went on strike. Transporting me to AIIMS evidently represented hardships above and beyond their normal call of duty. Prolonged negotiations and a lengthy stint in the ladies' loo ensued. I finally made the trip in the Old Man's Mercedes.

Given the circumstances, a personal welcome from the AIIMS Director would have been welcome and appropriate. Instead, I found myself deposited in an empty lobby – the doctors and staff had gone on a flash strike hearing of the patient headed their way. I am an understanding man and I shall refrain from any cheap shots about the Hippocratic Oath.

One junior resident had been deputed to disinfect me in view of my efforts with Sikander. This he did with a hosepipe and something that smelled like phenyl. I had no prior warning and was doused before I could react. He handed me a slip of paper with a room number and disappeared. Dripping phenyl, I made my way to my assigned room.

Mary was at the nurses' station but turned away when she saw me approaching. No giggles for Swami this time.

Being holed up at AIIMS was all very nice but I had files to deal with, matters to attend to, a country to run. Instead I was stuck in the modern day equivalent of a Red Fort dungeon reserved for surplus princes.

I called the Old Man. He was on no account to be disturbed.

I called my office. Too busy to answer the phone, of course.

This, then, was what it had all come to. Shunned by all and alone in a gilded cage. My services to the country unappreciated. My years of engaging in the most rarefied reaches of policy making washed away in a flood of cheap phenyl.

Days passed.

Like that stressed-out steel girder, I was bowed and bent, no longer able to bear the burden of office. Forget office. Even the burden of life was getting to be a bit much.

There was a commotion outside one afternoon. The Old Man walked in, attended to by the paraphernalia that surrounds every senile politician.

'You are improving, Swami?'

'I was perfectly all right, sir. I didn't ask to be admitted to hospital.'

He ignored me and inspected the bathroom.

'Bathroom clean I see. No more commotion with your motion?'

'There was, and is, nothing wrong with my motion, sir,' I said with all the dignity I could muster. Striped pajamas are not really conducive to dignified conversation and even if I had been warned of the Old Man's coming, my blazer had not survived its encounter with phenyl.

'Good, good. Too much diarrhoea is not good for your health. You must look after your health.

What you need is a position with less stress. When you are better, I shall personally find you a suitable position. Now you need rest. No excitement for you. So take good rest.'

He exited along with his accompanying paraphernalia.

I turned to the TV, desultorily taking in the news. Cock-ups all the way up and down the line: the country was going down the tubes and the one man who could do something about it was wearing striped pajamas and desultorily watching TV. If they didn't want me, well, that was their headache and I didn't really care.

Preoccupied, I didn't see the Old Man come in. Alone.

'Beta, shabhash. I wanted to thank you for saving my job, and Kashmir. Achhcha kiya toone.' He spoke in a conspiratorial whisper. 'I told them I was going to the bathroom, so I better go back before there is a parliamentary inquiry into my disappearance. Anyway, I've brought a present for you.'

He handed me a nicely wrapped package before sneaking out.

I spent the afternoon staring at the package and thinking dark thoughts. Late that evening, curiosity got the better of me and I ripped off the packaging. It was a DVD.

Yes, the Choli Girl herself. Digitally altered, of course.

Post Script

Prime Minister Motwani suffered a heart attack one evening while watching his favourite movie. He was rushed to the AIIMS where he lapsed into a coma. He continues his comatose existence at great public expense in the AIIMS ICU.

A secret ISI inquiry into the disastrous performance of the Pakistani cricket team led to the uncovering of the Motwani–Shah bet. Shah and his family were exiled as a result of the coup that followed and took up residence in a sea-side villa in Mogadishu. His attempts at getting Harrah's to set up a casino in Mogadishu have not borne fruit.

Sikandar escaped from Delhi zoo during a karmachari's strike and ended up as a seekh kabab in an Old Delhi restaurant.

An Empowered Group of Secretaries, after due deliberation, decided that the Super Sofa be displayed in the National Museum alongside the historic red carpet. Difficulties in getting the sofa into the museum meant that it was stored in a shed outside while another Empowered Technical

296 • *The Goat, the Sofa and Mr Swami*

Committee pondered the alternatives. Over an exceptionally cold winter, some watchmen looking to ward off the chill consigned this bit of history to the flames. A CBI inquiry is under way.

Mr Swami reverted to his state and has been posted as Director General of the Poultry Directorate in the Animal Husbandry Department of the Government of Bihar. He holds the rank of Secretary to the Government and is entitled to an air-conditioned, chauffeur-driven Ambassador car. A DVD player has been installed in the car on Mr Swami's instructions.

Thanks

—•◆•—

First and foremost to my parents for everything that a son can thank his parents for, and so much more.

To Kamini for putting up with her brother's trans-generational leg pulling.

To Raja for fun, laughter, good cheer and encouragement over so many years.

To Soumitra and Huma for the home away from home and for not laughing even when it was warranted.

To Suresh Mathur, english teacher extraordinary.

To Nandita Aggarwal for taking this from an unsolicited email to a completed book painlessly and with good humour.

And to you, dear reader, for having made it this far with, I hope, a few laughs on the way.